Paperback ISBN: 978-1-959955-44-3
Hardback ISBN: 978-1-959955-31-3

Published by Landon Hail Press

Author's Note

AFTER A LIFETIME engaging in various roles in human services and interacting with people of all ages, backgrounds, and ethnicities, I have identified some common themes that have proved helpful to many. These themes are concepts and ideas that pertain practically to our life's struggles.

As I have explained these themes to others, they often say, "I never thought about that before. I wish I had."

I have also heard others say they didn't see people like themselves in the books they were reading. They found it difficult to relate to the characters in the story.

So, I decided to incorporate these themes and teachings into a story. I also wanted the story to be applicable and relatable to anyone. As I pondered on how to accomplish this, I began to realize that the main characters in the story needed to be stripped of ethnicity and gender, so the reader could fill in the blanks. I also determined that I should remain anonymous and donned the moniker A Nic Dotal.

This process was more difficult than I realized. Telling a story without pronouns is quite a challenge. It was also a little frustrating, because I had to repeat the character's names throughout.

Consequently, if this becomes a little tedious and redundant at times, I apologize. I couldn't figure out a better way to accomplish this.

I also decided to make the story allegorical, with some ancient symbology tossed in for good measure.

I hope that you like *A Story of N E Wan* and that the concepts contained within will help you avoid certain hardships in your life. I also hope that these lessons can inform you as you work through any tough times you are currently experiencing.

After reading this work, maybe you, too, will be able to say, "I am N E Wan."

Chapter 1

N E WAN AWOKE with a start and sensed that something was wrong, deadly wrong. N E stepped from the bed into knee-deep water.

Oh, no! What's happening? thought N E.

"The boat is sinking! Abandon ship!" came a voice from the outside.

N E Wan stumbled through the water to the door and opened it. More water rushed in from the corridor, pushing N E back into the room. Half-swimming, N E moved out of the door, up the hallway, and out to the deck of the boat.

It was pitch-dark outside. People were screaming and jumping from the railing.

Climbing the railing, N E heard the cries and panic in the voices all around. N E leapt from the railing and seemed to drop for an eternity. N E Wan hit the water and descended deep into the sea.

Thrashing about with lungs about to explode, N E finally broke the surface of the water and began to gasp for air. The sounds of people calling for help continued to echo in the darkness.

N E Wan began to swim away from the sinking vessel, and the voices began to fade. As the boat continued to sink, it made a metallic moaning sound. Then, it disappeared under the waves.

Trying to stay afloat, N E began to grow tired and exhausted. As N E struggled, one of N E's hands struck a solid object. It was a large, wooden box bobbing up and down in the water.

N E quickly grabbed hold and climbed up onto it, while trying to keep it balanced, and avoid capsizing the crate. Finding the sweet spot and lying down on the top, N E Wan lapsed into unconsciousness.

As N E Wan awoke, the sun had begun to rise. Looking around and seeing no one, N E wondered, *Where is everyone? Am I alone on the ocean?*

Floating on the wooden crate with nothing but water to the horizon, N E tried to come to grips with this new situation. Then, slowly, not wanting it to fill with water, N E loosened a plank from the crate.

Reaching into the gap and feeling a handle, N E began to pull on it. Through the gap emerged a suitcase. The crate seemed to be filled with luggage. Carefully, N E took out each bag, examined it, and removed any needed items, before the bag was replaced, to keep the crate from capsizing.

Clothing, a hat, sunscreen, candy, granola bars, and several plastic bags of medicine bottles and toiletries were gleaned from the baggage. N E was lucky to have found some food. Yet, there was no fresh water. N E was surrounded by miles and miles of water but couldn't drink any of it.

Using the clothing to make a shield from the sun, N E began to smear sunblock on any exposed skin, and then N E organized the various supplies. Next, N E Wan prepared for what might become a long ordeal on the ocean.

N E took a plastic container and filled it with sea water. Then, N E covered the container with a tent of small plastic sheets N E had assembled. The sheets were connected so they sloped downward to another empty container. A fresh-water collection contraption was now complete. N E hoped the salt water would evaporate and collect on the bottom of the plastic sheeting. The salt would remain in the first container. If luck held out, fresh water would be running down the plastic sheeting and into the empty bowl.

Sure enough, as the day became warmer, the water evaporated, and droplets formed on the bottom of the plastic sheets. As the pool built up, the water began to run down the slope and into the empty container. Now there was a small supply of fresh water. N E Wan loudly celebrated this life-saving victory.

With survival now a possibility, N E Wan began to calm down and reflect on why N E had taken this trip in the first place. N E contemplated all of the events and circumstances that had led up to this moment.

Before embarking on this voyage, N E had spent more than a year caring for a mother's needs as illness overtook her. N E Wan was the only person there for her. Day after day, N E met her every need, even though it meant sacrificing N E's own future plans, hopes, and dreams. N E wouldn't leave her side and felt the immense pain and grief of watching this woman, who had always seemed invincible, waste away.

When the end finally arrived, N E grieved yet also felt a sense of relief. Then, N E felt guilty for feeling relieved.

Eventually, N E had to deal with the fallout of what remained of a mother's life. What to keep? What to give away? N E began going through box after box of memorabilia and old photographs.

Then, N E found a box that would change everything. A box full of N E's father's memories. Wondering what had become of this father, whom N E had hardly known as a child, N E began to go through the effects N E's mother had kept about him. N E read his letters and his journal, scouring every page for information about him and what had happened to him.

The story slowly began to unfold of a husband leaving on a trip. His tearful goodbye. A trip that would change everything for the family. N E pieced together what he had left of a ship. There were also the details of the route the ship would take. Then, there was nothing.

Eventually, after all of the chores of closing out a lifetime of experiences and possessions were concluded, N E Wan had an idea.

What if my father is out there somewhere? Maybe I can find him.

While planning the trip and making the arrangements for passage on a boat, N E decided to follow the same route. *I just have to find my father*, N E Wan remembered thinking, while sitting on the crate in the middle of the ocean. The mysterious disappearance had led to more questions than answers. Finally, N E had taken a boat trip to the last known location of N E Wan's missing father.

Now, disaster had struck, and N E was stranded in the middle of the sea. N E pondered, *Was this a fool's errand? Maybe I may never know what happened. None of this may even matter, if I don't figure out how to survive this.*

N E lay down on a bed of clothing and fell asleep. Sometime after midnight, a wave splashed on the crate, and N E Wan awoke. Sitting up and looking around, N E saw that the moon was shining brightly and reflecting off the surface of the water.

Using a towel salvaged from the crate to dry off, N E felt a strange feeling of calm settle in. N E sat up and looked at the beauty and the lights.

"Lights? What lights? On the horizon. Lights!" shouted N E.

Now, with a surge of adrenaline, N E pulled a plank from the crate. Then, after rummaging through the baggage, N E began to piece together a plan. N E assembled two makeshift paddles. After a few failed efforts, the paddles actually worked.

N E began to paddle toward the lights. It was a long distance to go, so N E alternated between resting, drinking, eating, and paddling. The lights soon began to come closer and closer. N E's muscles began to burn, yet there was no slowing down.

Suddenly, the crate came to a dead stop in the water. N E was thrust forward and thrown into the sea. By swimming and using the energy of the waves, N E continued to move toward the lights.

Soon, the water started to become warmer, the waves started to crest, and the sound of the waves crashing on a shoreline gave N E hope.

N E Wan's feet touched a sandy bottom, and N E began to crawl through the surf. N E collapsed on a beach and fell into an exhausted sleep.

N E Wan was awakened by a strange sensation. N E's eyes began to open. Squinting into sunlight, N E saw a silhouette. Someone was standing there, poking N E with a stick.

A voice said, "You don't look so good. You okay? You look like a drowned rat."

"Am I alive? What is this place? Where am I? Who are you?" asked N E Wan.

"Well, it looks like you're alive, though a little worse for wear. You seem to have a strand of seaweed behind your ear. What is this place, you ask? This place is an island. Yes, you have washed up on the shore of the Island of Status Quo. The other answers can wait," replied the voice. "We need to get you out of the sun and cleaned up a bit."

Kneeling in the sand, the stranger removed the sea plants then helped N E Wan off the beach and over to what looked to be a three-sided bamboo hut with a palm frond roof. N E collapsed into what turned out to be a very comfortable, makeshift chair.

With some fresh water to wash away the sand and the sea, N E cleaned up and then rose to change into some clothing stacked nearby.

This stranger has thought of everything, thought N E Wan.

There was another chair nearby and a table with earthen and bamboo receptacles arranged on top. Now, feeling safe and starting to relax, N E looked around at the beautiful panorama of palm trees, turquoise clear water, and a deep-blue sky.

"Here, have some of my famous elixir and some dried fruits," said the stranger, handing N E a hollowed-out coconut and a woven plate made of palm fronds.

As N E ate hungrily and began gulping down the liquid, the stranger responded, "Hey, slow down. You'll make yourself sick and make a mess of my wonderful hideaway."

"What is this?" asked N E, now slowly drinking.

"That, my new friend, is a special recipe of coconut milk and some other secret ingredients. Yes, secret ingredients. I like secrets. Yes, once you get to know me, you'll find that I have many, many secrets," answered the stranger.

For some time, they sat quietly, listening to the surf and admiring the wonderful view. After feeling a bit more oriented to the surroundings, N E Wan said, "So, this is an island. The Island of Status Quo. What an odd name. And, if I may ask, who are you?"

Smiling broadly and looking rather pleased, the stranger replied, "I, my new friend, am called A Nic Dotal. You are very fortunate that I found you washed up on the beach. You may not have fared as well, if you were discovered by someone else. You see, there are only a few of us inhabiting this island, but not everyone is as hospitable and amenable as I."

Trying to take all of this in, N E Wan sat for a moment longer and then said, "Thank you for helping me. It does appear that it has been my good fortune to be in your company today. It is very nice to meet you, A Nic Dotal. My name is N E Wan." Then added, after a slight pause, "You say there are others on this island, as well?"

"Yes," replied A Nic Dotal, while looking at N E Wan with curiosity. "You will meet them soon enough, I am sure. You see, not much happens of interest, since we are so few here, and news travels fast. I am sure everyone will want to meet you to size you up."

"Size me up?" asked N E Wan. "What does that mean?"

"Oh, never you mind for now. There will be plenty of time for all of that. Now, you rest up, and let's just enjoy this wonderful scenery and each other's company," answered A Nic Dotal.

After a time, N E looked over at this new acquaintance and noticed that A Nic Dotal was looking back and smiling.

"Is something amusing?" N E Wan inquired.

"More like a bittersweet memory," replied A Nic Dotal. "You remind me of someone, and I was simply reminiscing. Yes, you may not be the only one who is fortunate, this fine day."

Then, rising and stretching, A Nic Dotal said, "I must take my leave for a short while. I have a few errands that need attending. So, for now, rest, relax, and walk on the beach. I will return when I am able."

With that, A Nic Dotal walked into the trees and out of sight. N E Wan continued to sit, thinking about all that had just happened.

What a strange trip this has been. Was this just a bump in the road? Or is the quest to find my missing father at an end? Was all of this effort and hardship for naught? Maybe just being alive is the best for now. Yet, it is a beautiful place to be stranded. There is also the good fortune of meeting a friendly stranger.

N E Wan rose from the chair and began to stroll casually down the beach. Looking ahead, N E noticed something in the sand. A sand dollar! A large, mostly perfect sand dollar. N E decided to set it down and pick it up on the way back.

Then, N E noticed another beautiful shell. Then, N E saw another shell and another. N E set each of the shells higher up on the beach, beyond the water, so they could be retrieved later.

Gazing up at the blue sky and smelling the sea air, N E thought, *That elixir was refreshing and invigorating!*

N E continued down the beach and eventually came to where a large river emptied into the sea. N E Wan could go no farther on the sand and turned to go back to the hut.

A large wave crashed right in front of N E. As the water receded, there, in the sand, was a conch shell. It was orange and white, with a spiny base and spiral design. N E picked it up and walked away from the water.

N E lifted the shell, held it to one ear, and expected to hear the sound of the sea. Instead, N E Wan's eyes flew open. N E stumbled back and fell on the sand.

Sitting in the sand and staring at the shell, N E's mouth dropped open in amazement.

"Did that shell just speak to me?" N E Wan asked to no one in particular.

Crawling slowing forward, N E examined the shell from all sides. Next, N E picked up the shell and held it to one ear.

"Yes," replied a voice from shell. "The shell is speaking to you."

"How?"

"Not sure."

"Not sure about what?"

"Not sure how the shell is speaking to you."

"Why?"

"Why what?"

"Why is a conch shell speaking to me?"

"No idea. Who are you?"

"My name is N E Wan."

Silence.

"Hello?"

"Yes, still here. Just taken aback. Give me a moment to collect my thoughts."

"Thoughts? A shell that can speak and has thoughts?"

"Okay, fine. Maybe I am as surprised as you."

"I doubt that. But it is kind of amazing and fun."

"What is?"

"Having a shell that can talk and has thoughts. That is really wild."

"Well, yes, it is very nice for me, also. It has been a long while since I spoke with anyone."

"That's funny."

"What's funny?"

"You haven't spoken to anyone, and my name is N E Wan, so now you have. Both, I mean."

"I'm confused."

"Never mind."

N E Wan stood for a moment, looking at the conch shell, then took the shell and the other shells and returned to the hut, where N E stacked them on the table.

Then, N E Wan sat in the comfortable chair and fell asleep. Soon, there was the jabbing again. Slowly opening one eye, N E saw the stick.

"Why do you keep poking me with that stick?" N E asked.

"I like this stick," replied A Nic Dotal. "I take it with me everywhere I go. I sleep with this stick. This is a wonderful stick! Plus, it is really good for poking people. My, my, look at these colorful shells." A Nic Dotal began to pick them up and examine them.

"I had the strangest dream," mused N E Wan. "I dreamed that I picked up that conch shell and put it to my ear. Then, it started talking to me. We had a conversation."

A Nic Dotal picked up the conch shell and held it to one ear.

A voice said, "*If someone says something better than you, make fun of them.*"

A Nic Dotal set the shell back on the table and stepped backward, eyes wide and mouth open, then whispered, "Maybe we are in the same dream."

"No way!" exclaimed N E Wan. "You heard it, too?"

"A talking shell," wondered A Nic Dotal aloud. "This is a marvel indeed! But, nonetheless, we will need to address this wonder sometime later. For now, I have made arrangements for you. You will have a place to stay and your other needs met. So, let's go and get you settled."

Chapter 2

USING A MAKESHIFT cloth bag, N E Wan
collected the shells, carefully placed them in the bag,
and then followed A Nic Dotal away from the beach
hut and through the trees. Soon, they came upon a
well-worn pathway and followed it for some time.

The air was hot and wet with humidity. N E was
soon sweating and uncomfortable. Eventually, the
trees began to clear, and they came upon a large
open area.

As they entered a small collection of thatched-
roof huts, they found people gathered together.
They all wore loose garments that looked to have
been brightly colored at one time, but were now
faded and worn. The people were mostly quiet and
subdued.

"You must be our new arrival," said one of the
group, stepping forward. His clothes were brightly
colored and much less worn than the others around
him. "My name is Art, and you are N E Wan."

"Yes," replied N E Wan. "News does travel fast
here."

"Come," said Art, waving for N E to enter the
small village. "Welcome to the Village of

Subjugation. We don't have much space right now, but we have made room for you in a storage hut. You will stay there."

They walked over to a small bamboo structure with a palm-frond roof and a sandy floor. N E Wan entered and set down the bag of shells. There was a woven mat rolled out in the corner.

A woman stooped at the doorway and entered the hut. "My name is Sue. I would like to show you around this little settlement." This woman, like Art, wore brightly colored, less-worn clothing.

"Thank you. That would be nice," replied N E.

"What's this?" Sue asked, picking up the sand dollar. "A collection of shells. How quaint." Then, picking up the conch shell, she began to examine it. "What an unusual shell." She held the shell up to her ear in a mocking manner.

Then her eyes opened wide in amazement as the voice from the shell said,

"You are not right simply because you can prove someone else wrong."

Sue quickly set the shell back with the others. To N E Wan, she seemed a bit rattled and less in control. Then, she stood up, straightened her clothing, took and deep breath, exhaled, and then said, "Time to go."

They exited the hut. The rest of the people seemed to have dispersed. A Nic Dotal reached out and took N E Wan's hand, held it for a moment, and then bid them farewell, exiting the village walking off into the trees.

"This way," motioned Sue as she walked through the village. "Our little group provides all of the food for the rest of the people on the island." Then, pointing to a wet area, she added, "This is where we grow taro. I see the look of confusion on your face. Taro is a root vegetable. It is starchy and can be prepared in various ways. We can also cook the leaves, a good source of vitamins. This plant provides a lot of good nutrition we need here on the Island of Status Quo."

Walking farther, they came upon a grove of trees. Up to this point, N E Wan had mostly seen bamboo and palm trees.

"These are breadfruit trees," Sue explained. "Again, I see that look. These produce fruit about the size of a grapefruit. They are tasty and can also be prepared and served in various dishes. All around us are coconut palms. I'm sure you know what a coconut is," she added in a dismissive tone. "And, finally, over here, we have bananas. So, as you can imagine, there is much to do around here. We will be putting you to work right away. Then, once you get your bearings and start pulling your weight, we can look into training you to fish and get other seafood."

N E was taken aback by these new plants. There was also a strange feeling about Sue. *Was she being condescending? Was N E just being overly sensitive?* They returned to the village and arrived at the storage hut and entered.

N E Wan asked, "Excuse me, Sue. What is your last name?"

Stopping and turning, Sue replied, "Oh, I see. Yes. My last name is Perior."

"Oh," said N E Wan. "Your name is Sue Perior. And the man who met us earlier. His name was Art?"

"Yes, that's right. Art Official. He and I are in charge here," replied Sue. "Now we need to get you some work clothes and get you to work." Having said this, she stooped through the door and walked away.

N E Wan lay down on the mat and fell asleep. In what seemed to be a very short period, that feeling of being poked with a stick returned. N E Wan's eyes slowly opened, and N E began looking around.

A woman was poking N E with a stick. "Wake up, sleepy head. There's work to be done. I've brought you some work clothes and a hat."

The woman was one of the people whom N E had seen earlier, at the entrance to the village. N E arose and began to change into the faded, worn work clothes, setting the clothing from A Nic Dotal aside.

"My name is N E Wan. And you are?"

"My name is Viola," replied the woman. "You will need to wear a hat."

"That's a very nice name. I like that," replied N E Wan. "What is your last name?"

"Ated. My last name is Ated," answered the woman.

"Oh," said N E Wan. "What work are we planning to do today?"

"Today, we are picking bunches of bananas," answered Viola. "It is hard work, because the bunches are large and heavy. It also rains here at least once a day. This makes the bunches and the pathways wet and slippery. So be careful."

As the day progressed, N E Wan learned about bananas. There was much emphasis placed on handling the very sharp machete that was used to sever the bunches from the plant and in determining which bunches to harvest and which to leave. Viola was correct about the weight and the hauling off the large bunches: it was exhausting.

She was also correct about the rain. On the one hand, the rain was a welcome relief to the heat. On the other hand, the heavy bananas were even more difficult to handle. To N E, the day seemed to last forever.

At several points during the day, N E noticed bright colors near the tree line. Turning to look, Art and Sue were found to be watching the workers from a distance. They were still wearing the nice clothes. They didn't seem to be joining in on the work being done.

Finally, after what seemed to be a lifetime, a bell rang. The workday was over. Viola Ated and N E Wan walked to a pathway and started back to the village. Soon, the pathway had many more people than had N E Wan had seen in the village earlier. N E noticed their worn clothes and downcast faces as they walked. Also evident was the presence of older people and children, who were included in the work groups.

N E Wan could hardly wait to get back, get something to eat, and go to bed. Yet, when they arrived at the village, there were tables assembled and fires with cookpots at the edge of the village, near the trees.

"Now we process the produce and the fish," said Viola.

N E Wan was astounded and gasped, "What? More work?"

"Yes," replied Viola. "This all needs to be prepared, so it doesn't go to waste."

N E assisted Viola throughout the afternoon. The work area was shaded by palm-frond panels on bamboo poles. Yet, with the fires burning plus cooking the greens in cauldrons and the sticky humid atmosphere, the heat was nearly unbearable.

Eventually, the day's renderings were chopped, cut, gutted, smoked, and cooked. N E Wan worked to clean up the area. Then, the bell rang for dinner.

Extremely fatigued, N E could hardly keep from falling into the woven plate brimming with food.

The fare seemed to be from the day's harvest. It tasted fresh and good.

"Do you always eat like this?" N E asked with a yawn.

"Yes," replied Viola. "This is what we eat every day for breakfast, lunch, and dinner."

"This isn't so bad. I like it."

"This is good food," Viola said. "It is tasty enough. But it isn't the best food that we harvest."

"What happens to the best food?" asked N E.

"It all goes to Self Center. See the crates over by the entrance to the village? Soon, people will transport the food, clothing, and other supplies from here to Self Center."

"What in the world is Self Center?" N E asked.

"Self Center is the home of the ones who run the island. They are in charge. We must do what they say. They always get the best of everything. The best homes, the best place on the island, the best clothing, and the best food." Viola scowled. "That is the home of Art Official and Sue Perior. They, in turn, work for Euphoria, Melancholia, and their two grown children. They are in charge of everything and everyone on the island. You have yet to meet most of them. They also have another child, who lives nearby." As she said this, she looked sad and defeated.

"How did all of this come to be?" asked N E Wan. "Why do these few people run everything?"

Viola replied, "Our grandparents used to live on the island in peace and harmony, as did their grandparents. Then, many years ago, there was a storm. After the storm, a different group of people came to the island on lifeboats. They said that their boat sank. The local islanders took pity on them, helped them, and took care of them. As time progressed, they began to change the way things were done. Our parents tried to confront them, but they were not successful. The visitors became aggressive and threatening. One man was even killed. We believe they murdered him."

Hearing this, N E Wan become quite concerned. Apparently, there was much more to learn about this island and its inhabitants. What Viola had described was not right. This was not how people should treat other people.

After the meal, N E worked to clean up the area and make preparations for the following morning. Then, N E Wan returned to the hut, dead tired and barely able to walk. Finally making it through the door, N E looked around at the meager accommodations and noticed the conch shell.

N E picked up the shell and lay down on the mat. The next thing N E recalled was being poked by a stick as someone said it was time to get up.

Rising from the mat, sore and still tired from the previous day, N E Wan stumbled out of the hut and over to an area where people were washing. Next came breakfast. Sure enough, it was the same meal as the night before. Then, the bell rang for work.

As the days passed, N E continued the routine of work then cooking and preparing the produce and seafood. Soon, N E's body began to acclimate to the heat and humidity. Although, the work did not become easier, N E's strength and stamina seemed to increase. N E had never done physical labor like this, but there seemed to be a sort of spiritual connection to the daily routines and rhythms. There was a strange sense of order and purpose, something N E Wan had not felt before.

N E soon learned to cultivate and harvest various crops. N E took much satisfaction in learning about plants and their care. N E also began helping with the production of clothing and jewelry, utilizing the various island plants to produce loose-fitting garments. N E learned to make the various brightly colored dyes, which N E found interesting and brought out a creative side in N E Wan. Using shells and other colorful objects to make jewelry also piqued N E's interest.

As N E grew stronger and more competent, N E Wan earned the acceptance and friendship of the many coworkers and others in the village. One day, N E was assigned to the boats and traps. This proved to be another fascinating learning experience.

N E Wan found it fascinating, how they maneuvered the boats, and N E came to understand more about the fish and the sea creatures that inhabited the shallows around the island. Even the makeshift life vests were innovative and interesting.

Yet, N E Wan felt a nagging discomfort with the whole situation. N E's sightings of those in the brightly colored clothing continued, the ones who didn't do any of the work. They were clean and well groomed. They remained distant and aloof. The majority of the food and supplies still left the village each night to go to Self Center.

One evening, after entering the hut, N E Wan noticed the bag of shells in the corner that N E had collected on N E's very first day on the island. The bag had somehow gone unnoticed since then.

N E Wan also recalled that A Nic Dotal had not been seen since that day on the beach. N E had liked A Nic Dotal and hoped nothing was amiss.

N E sat on the mat with the bag and took out the shells one by one. There was the sand dollar, and there was the conch, the strange shell that had a voice inside. *Was that just a dream? Did that really happen?* N E began to examine the large, beautiful shell and then slowly brought it up to listen.

"It's been a while," spoke the voice in the shell.

"So, it wasn't a dream or my imagination? There really is a voice in this shell," said N E Wan, while holding the shell and looking at it with wonder. Then, N E held it up to one ear and listened again.

"Nope, you weren't dreaming," replied the voice. "Haven't heard from you in a while. You doing okay? Hanging in there?"

"There is a lot of work to do around here," N E answered. "At first, it was overwhelming. It took me a long time to get used to the heat and the long days. But now, I feel much better. I am learning so many wonderful new skills, and there is so much to know about plants and the ocean. I am even getting pretty good at working on the boats."

"Sounds like you are handling all of this quite well," replied the voice. "How are the villagers treating you? Are you being accepted into the group?"

"Oh, yes! My first day, a woman named Viola Ated helped me, and she has been a very good friend ever since. Many of the other people in the village have taken me under their wing, to teach me and help me. For instance, Vic and Tim Ization are really nice and teaching me so much about the ocean."

"My goodness," replied the voice. "You seem to have met these changes and challenges head-on. Having made so many friends in such a short time is evidence of having a good character."

"Why, thank you, voice from the shell!" N E laughed.

"You are very welcome," answered the shell.

After sitting for a moment, N E confessed, "There is something that has been bothering me. A group of people seem to live in a place called Self Center. They come by now and again. They are sent the best food, clothing, and supplies, but they don't do any work."

"Hmmm," replied the voice. "I was wondering when you were going to get around to those folks. They are not nice people. I strongly suggest you keep your distance from them."

"How can they get away with all of this?" asked N E. "Why doesn't somebody stop them?"

"Some people have gone up against them. They are very skilled at the art of subjugation. So, no one has yet to succeed."

"Subjugation? This is the Village of Subjugation. What exactly is the meaning of the word?"

The voice responded, "Subjugation is a word that describes what results when one group of people takes dominion or control of another group of people."

N E thought about that for a moment. "You said that this was a skill or an art of the people from Self Center. How so?"

The voice explained, "Subjugation involves coercion. This is where one person identifies characteristics in another person or group of people that make them vulnerable to threat.

"This threat can be physical in nature. One person may be stronger or larger than another. The threat can also be a willingness of one person to injure another, or worse. The physical threat can also be used against a loved one or someone's possessions. The skill and artistry come into play through the ability to be convincing. They may demonstrate their willingness to be violent. Then, going forward, they use intimidation to keep this fear alive in the other people.

"The threat is not limited to physical or bodily harm. A person can be threatened mentally and emotionally, as well. This can involve the continual insulting or demeaning of another. When one person identifies what another values, a physical feature of the person or a skill they have acquired, then they can use these characteristics as a weapon against that other person. They mock and belittle them. They also use these tactics to turn others against them.

"When successful, the aggressive person creates a social dynamic that has them in a position of authority and dominion. They say, 'I am better than you. Our group is superior to yours. You are lucky I let you have what little you do. You are indebted to us. Don't resist us, because you have much to lose if you do. We can make you very sorry if we want to, so don't cross us.'

"Upon achieving this state of affairs, it is necessary to maintain this subjugation. Thus, it is important to establish domination as the status quo." The shell fell silent.

"This is very enlightening and upsetting," said N E Wan. "It explains so much of what I see going on around here. The people don't even question. Or maybe, if they do have questions, they are too afraid to ask because of what might happen."

"Yes," answered the voice. "It takes a lot of courage to stand up against people like this. They can be very dangerous. They like what they have, and they will go to great lengths to keep it."

Yawning, N E Wan thanked the voice in the shell then put all of the shells back in the bag. Then, lying back onto the mat, N E Wan feel into a deep sleep.

Chapter 3

AS THE DAYS PASSED, N E Wan continued the routine. The learning of new skills, gaining the acceptance of the other villagers, and noticing the brightly colored clothing near the tree line became a daily experience.

One particular day, as N E was climbing down from a coconut palm, Sue Perior was waiting at the base of the tree.

She said, "Well, well, well. It looks like you are working out better than expected. You know, I really didn't have much hope for you in the beginning. When A Nic Dotal told us you had washed up on the beach, I really didn't know what to think.

"Anyhow, I need you to transport the crates at the entrance to the village tonight. So, make sure you are ready and on time. After you finish all your usual work, that is."

Something about Sue Perior's tone really infuriated N E Wan. But, remembering the advice from the voice in the shell, N E Wan simply nodded. Then, Sue walked away.

N E did the assigned work for the remainder of the day, then N E Wan went to the entrance of the village that evening. Standing beside one of the crates was A Nic Dotal.

"Greetings, N E Wan!" exclaimed A Nic Dotal. "It warms my heart to see you again. I have heard nothing but wonderful reports of your progress and your work ethic. I am so pleased that you are well."

N E smiled in return. Although N E had been somewhat confused by the absence of A Nic Dotal up to this point, N E was pleased to meet A Nic again, nonetheless. Then, N E asked, "What, exactly, am I supposed to do with these crates?"

"Oh yes, the crates," replied A Nic Dotal. "Let me help you. We pick them up and put them on this cart."

So, N E Wan and A Nic Dotal loaded the crates on the cart. Then, N E asked, "Now what?"

"Now, you pull the cart up the pathway to Self Center."

As N E began to pull the cart, A Nic Dotal pushed the cart from the rear.

N E was surprised by this. "I didn't think people from your group did any work around here."

A Nic Dotal responded, "First of all, I would suggest you not say things like that aloud. It will not turn out well for you. Secondly, I don't belong to a group."

N E asked, "You don't live in Self Center?"

"Oh, heavens no. I have my own home off by myself. I also like to go to the beach hut, where we first met." A Nic Dotal gave the cart a shove then continued, "Although I came to the island with the others on the lifeboats, I do not consider myself to be one of their group. I live alone in my own place.

"Now that you are going to Self Center for the first time, I wanted to accompany you and give you some advice and companionship. You will be delivering food and supplies to each of the residences there. I strongly suggest you do not speak unless spoken to. You will be met by Mister Ection and Miss Demeanour. They are the adult children of Euphoria and Melancholia.

"They are charged with keeping order on the island. They can be quite unpleasant, if crossed. They will be looking for any sign that you are capable of defying them. So, don't show any sort of disagreement or noncompliance."

As they were walking up the path, several older people passed them on their way back to the village. After they had moved on, N E asked, "What were they doing at Self Center?"

A Nic Dotal answered, "They are the servants of the inhabitants there. They cook, clean, and wait on them. The older people are used as servants, because they aren't as productive in the other work."

N E said, "The more I learn about the inhabitants of Self Center, the less I like them."

"Best to keep those thoughts to yourself. And by the way, don't be sharing these thoughts in the village. Some of the other villagers use every opportunity to win favor with those in Self Center. They will betray your confidence in a heartbeat."

"Now I really am starting to get depressed," mumbled N E Wan.

They traveled on in silence for a while, until they reached the entrance to Self Center. The residences there were made of the same materials as the huts in the Village of Subjugation, but they seemed roomier and better built. Plants hung in baskets on the sides of the houses, and several large cages with birds were around the center square.

Behind Self Center, farther down the hill that rose from the center of the island, was a large, beautiful waterfall. Near Self Center was a pool that led to the edge of the waterfall. The potted plants made the place smell wonderful, and the songs of the birds gave a nice melodic quality to the place.

Two people, a man and a woman, approached them where they stood with the cart. They were very tall and had muscular builds. Their clothes were bright and immaculate. Instantly, N E Wan snapped out of this reverie and remembered where they really were.

The woman spoke as they approached. "Oh my, what an honor. The enigmatic A Nic Dotal has chosen to bless us with a visit."

Then, both walked up close and looked down their noses at N E Wan. The man said, "This must be the little sea urchin rescued by A Nic Dotal. Not much to look at. What's your name, urchin?"

N E looked up at the two. "My name is N E Wan, and I was very fortunate that A Nic Dotal found me washed up after the sinking of our boat."

At this, the two people exchanged a startled look.

The woman asked firmly, "Did you say your name was N E Wan? Hmmm. And A Nic Dotal has taken you under wing, so to speak? I hope this will not become a problem, A Nic Dotal."

A Nic Dotal smiled. "Why, of course this will not be any trouble at all. N E Wan is very productive and well liked in the village already."

The man stated, "Rest assured, we will be keeping an eye on this situation. Anyway, move along, and distribute the goods. Then, be off."

A Nic Dotal escorted N E Wan around Self Center as they distributed the goods. First, they came to the home of Art Official and Sue Perior.

Sue came to the doorway and said, "Well, it looks like you recruited help with your assignment, N E Wan. A Nic Dotal, you might actually become useful around here, if you keep this up."

Next, they came to a very large and well-appointed home. Two people came to the door. They, like the others, were well dressed, very clean, and well groomed. They also wore ornate beaded jewelry.

A Nic Dotal stepped forward and said, "Euphoria and Melancholia, this is N E Wan."

N E Wan, again, noticed a startled expression when saying the name, "N E Wan," and N E began to wonder, *What is so startling about my name?*

The one called Euphoria said boisterously, "Well, I don't think our new subject here will cause us any problems at all. I think everything is going to be just fine."

Melancholia spoke up, asking, "How can you even think that? The villagers give us nothing but trouble, all of the time. If we let them, they would devolve into utter chaos. And now, there's one more. I don't see anything good about this situation at all."

A Nic Dotal quickly said, "Well, it was nice seeing you again. We will distribute today's goods and be on our way."

In what seemed like no time at all, they were leaving Self Center and on the path back to the Village of Subjugation.

After they had walked silently for a while, A Nic Dotal said, "That went better than expected. By the way, do you still have that talking shell? I have often thought about it, since first meeting you."

"Why yes, I do still have the shell. You can talk to it when we get back," replied N E Wan.

"Oh, the shell lets you talk to it, as well?"

"Why, yes. I had an interesting conversation with it recently," N E said.

The two entered the village, put away the cart, then went to N E Wan's hut. N E pulled out the bag of shells and retrieved the conch shell.

A Nic Dotal took the shell and listened.

The voice in the shell said,

"Why come to a conclusion in the middle of the story?"

A Nic Dotal held the shell out, examined it, and then asked, "Voice in the shell, do you mind if I ask you some questions?"

Holding the shell to listen, all A Nic heard was the sound of the sea.

"No answer," said A Nic Dotal.

"That's odd," N E said. "I had a lengthy conversation with it."

A Nic Dotal put the shell on the mat on the floor and then left the hut. Turning just outside the door, A Nic Dotal bid N E Wan farewell and walked away.

N E picked up the conch shell and asked, "Why don't you want to talk to anyone else?"

The voice in the shell said, "I only like to talk to N E Wan, not anyone else. Have you been thinking about our last conversation?"

"Yes," replied N E. "I think about it all the time. I was thinking about it as I went to Self Center this evening. I met the inhabitants there."

"Well, I suppose it is fortunate we had the talk before you went there," said the voice. "What did you think of them?"

"After you explained about coercion and intimidation, I was able to identify some of their tactics. They stand close to you and tower over you. They speak in a stern manner. They also word their statements to influence your thinking. For instance, one said, 'Well, I don't think our new subject will cause any problems at all.'

"Firstly, they used the term subject to describe me. Then, they decided for me that I wasn't going to cause trouble. Instead of being intimidated, I became intrigued.

"A Nic Dotal said something that made me quite anxious. That when it involves the residents of Self Center, the villagers are not to be trusted. They will betray anyone in the village, if they think it will help them gain the favor of the others."

"Yes, this is wise counsel indeed," replied the voice. "The residents of Self Center have long cultivated the illusion that it is better to cooperate and support them than to go against them in any way.

"You will soon notice that the oppressors will express symbolic and congratulatory sentiments toward workers they feel may be gaining popularity or respect in the village. They also host celebrations where they seem generous. They allow the workers time off of work, and they give titles and awards to the most productive. This gives the workers the illusion of their generosity and benevolence, when in reality, everything they are given rightfully belonged to the workers in the first place."

"How do they get away with this?" asked N E. "Don't the workers see right through it?"

"Some of the older workers have witnessed the retaliation against those who did stand up for themselves in the past. A few did question them. They were met with stern rebuke, and the workers, as a group, were punished severely. One person was taken away and did not return.

"So, instead of realizing that they held all of the real power in the situation, the workers decided to accept the dominion of those from Self Center. They embraced the status quo. This is why you are being advised to be very careful with what you say and how you act, even in the village."

Having had a very long day, N E Wan thanked the voice in the shell and put it back in the bag. Then, N E lay down on the mat and fell asleep.

Chapter 4

TIME SEEMED TO PASS slowly on the Island of Status Quo. N E Wan continued to perform the various duties and, on occasion, delivered the supplies to Self Center.

N E's close friendship continued with Viola Ated. Yet, N E was very careful to keep any controversial opinions close to the vest.

Another friendship sprouted with Vic and Tim Ization. They were brothers who worked primarily with the boats and the seafood harvests. They had a vast knowledge of the currents and how to navigate the sea surrounding the island. They also understood sea life and how to harvest it.

They enthusiastically taught N E Wan how to best handle the crafts and to travel the waters around the island. There was much to learn about currents, the tides, and the various creatures in the sea. Certain species were edible, some were poisonous, and some were to be avoided all together. Yet, to N E, they were all wonderful and interesting. Being on the ocean and working with the boats was also very rewarding.

Each evening after work, N E continued to have regular conversations with the voice in the shell. Having an outlet to talk to concerning N E's frustrations and the abuses taking place on the island was something N E looked forward to. The voice seemed insightful and was very comforting.

A Nic Dotal was nowhere to be seen during this time. N E missed A Nic Dotal and wondered why A Nic remained absent. Yet, Art and Sue continued to appear at the tree line, making sure the work was being done. It seemed that their mere presence was enough to keep the work going.

One day, N E Wan awoke from a restful sleep. Working hard seemed to produce the best sleep. After awaking and washing up, N E met Viola for breakfast.

"Isn't it exciting?" she exclaimed.

"Well, you certainly seem excited," answered N E Wan.

"No, silly! Celebration Day is in three days!"

N E calmly replied, "Ah, Celebration Day. Celebration Day? What is that?"

"Celebration Day means we don't have to work that day. We must do more work leading up to that day, to make up for taking a day off, but on that day, we get to sleep in, then we have a big party. Art Official and Sue Perior also come down for an awards ceremony. It is so very exciting. I hope I win an award this year."

"That does sound exciting," said N E Wan.

"Well, you don't sound very excited," said Viola.

Recalling the previous advice, N E replied, "You caught me off guard. I guess I was a little distracted. Yes, it does sound exciting, and the awards sound really nice."

"Yes, the awards! I know I will get one this year!"

Fortunately, N E was assigned to the boats for the next three days, because the work load had been increased. There was more seafood to harvest each day, but N E enjoyed being out in the boats on the sea, so it didn't seem to matter much. N E Wan also enjoyed the company of Vic and Tim immensely.

The three days passed. N E was sleeping soundly when a familiar sensation gradually pulled away the slumber. Was that the poking of a stick? It had been a long while since the last poking of a stick.

Slowly opening one eye, Viola's face was right in N E's. Annoyed, N E Wan exclaimed, "I thought we were allowed to sleep in!"

"How can you sleep?" Viola giggled. "It's Celebration Day!"

Slowly, N E Wan arose and stepped outside. The workers were happily mingling with one another. The conversations were animated. The faces wore smiles, and laughter wafted throughout the village.

N E washed and went to breakfast. The food wasn't the usual fare. This was the good food, and it tasted wonderful.

Throughout the morning, N E was careful to fit in. Although the ruse was evident, that the people were being manipulated, N E smiled and went along with it. There would be much to discuss with the voice in the shell this evening.

It did seem odd that the workers were serving themselves the very food they had harvested and prepared for the past three days and were celebrating over it. N E Wan recalled how, earlier, the women who made the jewelry had been crafting the necklaces that would be awarded on Celebration Day. They did not find this paradoxical whatsoever. They were quite content, even joyous.

N E Wan smiled and continued to go along with the group.

Around midafternoon, the people began to gather at the entrance to the village. Soon, Art Official and Sue Perior emerged from the trees and entered the village. At their arrival, the people erupted in applause. This seemed to please them terrifically. However, Art and Sue kept their distance. There was not even a handshake. Just smiles and waves to the workers, who didn't seem to mind.

Eventually, Art held up his hands and the people became quiet. "I trust you are enjoying Celebration Day. As you know, we at Self Center take this time each year to acknowledge hard work and dedication. This year is no different. Thanks to all of your efforts this past year, we can now celebrate. For, you see, we have been watching, and we have chosen who will receive special recognition."

At this, the people applauded. They really did look excited. Viola was fidgeting beside N E Wan in anticipation.

Sue Perior stepped forward, holding the necklaces made by the workers a few days prior. She held up the jewelry, and the people cheered. She was obviously basking in the attention.

"Our great leaders, Euphoria and Melancholia, have asked me to express their great appreciation for your hard work and dedication."

Again, the people cheered and applauded. Observing this performance, N E wondered if there really was artistry in the domination of others.

Sue continued, "First, I would like to present the award for the most beautiful jewelry to Cam E Lione."

An older woman shyly stepped forward. The people cheered. Sue beamed as she put the necklace around the woman's neck. The very necklace the woman had finished making the day before. Yet, the woman seemed to be very moved by the award.

"Next," announced Sue, "we have the award for the most produce produced!" She laughed as this was said, and the people laughed as well. "The award goes to Gil Teaman!"

The crowd applauded as a younger man, whom N E Wan had often seen in the village, stepped forward. He was very muscular and did not make eye contact with Sue or the crowd. He seemed to be looking at the ground while he walked forward. N E Wan's mother used to call this "navel gazing." He accepted the award to the applause of the crowd.

Sue continued, "The next award goes to the worker with the best new recipe for island fare. This award goes to Viola Ated!"

Viola let out a scream that startled N E Wan and many of the people standing nearby. Sue seemed very pleased at this outcry of enthusiasm. Viola accepted the award then ran to N E, to display the necklace. Sue noticed this and whispered something to Art.

"Our last award goes to honor the best worker with the boats and seafood harvest."

As she said this, N E noticed Vic and Tim smiling. *Are they smiling at me?* N E Wan wondered.

"This award goes to N E Wan!" shouted Sue.

The crowd erupted in the loudest cheer of the day. N E Wan felt strangely moved by the appreciation.

Suddenly, time seemed to slow. N E slowly walked to Sue and accepted the award. Sue and Art were not smiling but seemed to be studying N E Wan's expression.

As N E Wan returned to the group, Vic and Tim were jumping up and down, clapping and smiling. Viola ran up, shouting, "We both won!"

Art Official quieted the group and said, "We look forward to another great year. We look forward to our next Celebration Day! We know that each and every one of you will continue to work hard."

Then, Art and Sue waved and left the village. N E Wan noticed other bright colors just inside the tree line. As Art and Sue walked up the path to Self Center, they were joined by Mister Ection and Miss Demeanour.

That evening, N E Wan joined the celebration and enjoyed the wonderful food. There was a camaraderie with these villagers. N E felt warm and accepted.

At the close of the evening, returning to the hut, N E removed the necklace and picked up the bag of shells, then lifted the conch shell and listened.

The shell said, "Congratulations. You should be very proud."

"I do feel proud. But the whole event is a sham. So, why do I feel proud? Why do I feel validated?" queried N E Wan.

The voice replied, "You feel validated and affirmed because you were. The event may be a sham. The motivation may be to control and dominate. Yet, the work itself was legitimate. The appreciation of your peers is genuine. So, enjoy it. You earned it.

"Also, understand that it is part of the strategy of domination. Using genuine praise is a tactic, yet it is fulfilling and rewarding, nonetheless. This is why they do it. People pushed beyond their limitations reach a point where they have nothing to lose. This desperation often leads to revolt. Therefore, it is important to those at Self Center to keep the workers compliant, and not to push them to the edge of their tolerance.

"This symbolic celebration is a social mechanism they use to give the illusion that they care about the people. They don't want to be seen for the monsters they are."

"It works," conceded N E. "I felt so wonderful today. They really pulled it off. Yet, I also felt conflicted. On the one hand, I recognized the ruse, and I was disgusted by it. On the other hand, I had a feeling of admiration for the cunning and their ability to execute such a sublime tactic."

The voice replied, "Yes, I hear what you are saying. It is a strange response that we can have. We can admire courage and audacity in someone we know is using and abusing others. Accomplishing evil is still an accomplishment. It leaves a sour taste in your mouth just to say it. Great human attributes can be employed for evil. We may feel admiration, but we must temper it with the recognition that the actions are destructive and wrong.

"We can learn from anyone. We must, however, remember that they are malicious and mean-spirited. There is an old saying that learning is like eating fish. You eat the meat and spit out the bones."

"That oddly makes sense." N E pondered this. "And how can you have a sour taste in your mouth? You are a shell. You don't have a mouth."

"Hmmm," replied the shell. "Aren't you getting tired?"

N E laughed, said good night to the voice in the shell, and then lay awake, running through the day's events and thinking.

Chapter 5

THE NEXT MORNING following Celebration Day was business as usual. Over the next several days, N E Wan was assigned to various tasks, including two deliveries to Self Center.

Other than falling out of the boat, nothing happened that was out of the ordinary. Vic did teach N E some new techniques with the life vests, which were made from common items found on the island, yet worked rather well at keeping one afloat.

One morning, while deep in sleep, a familiar sensation slowly coaxed N E Wan awake. "Is someone poking me with a stick?" N E asked aloud.

"I told you, I like this stick," replied a familiar voice.

N E Wan sat up and smiled at A Nic Dotal. "Maybe I should get myself a stick." N E laughed

"Maybe you should," responded A Nic Dotal. "Now, get up, sleepyhead. We have a big day ahead of us."

"What? No work today?"

"Not for you," A Nic Dotal replied. "Now, get up, get washed, have breakfast, and let's be on our way."

As N E Wan went through the usual morning ritual, the other villagers acted rather strangely. No one was used to having someone like A Nic Dotal in their midst. Then, the villagers seemed to be whispering amongst themselves, once they realized that N E Wan was not going to do any work that day.

N E felt relieved when they finally left the village. The day turned out to be a wonderful adventure, exploring the island. N E saw many new places and enjoyed not only a day off work, but a day with a dear friend.

First, they went to the beach where N E Wan had washed ashore. N E found some beautiful new shells there. Once again, on the beach, was a large sand dollar. After a walk along the sand, they relaxed in the bamboo hut, ate delicious fruits, and drank the mysterious elixir.

"How did you make this happen?" N E asked.

"The inhabitants of Self Center have taken a special interest in you," replied A Nic Dotal. "They are becoming suspicious. They are usually wary of anyone who stands out among the villagers.

"So, I met with Euphoria and Melancholia, and I assured them I would make a special effort to find out whether or not you had untoward ambitions. They seemed relieved to hear this. They hold me in high esteem, you see. What they don't know is that we are already friends, and I am simply giving you a day off of work."

N E Wan took a long drink of elixir and asked, "Do you think they know that I can see through their ways of dominating the villagers?"

"Hmmm," replied A Nic Dotal. "I think they sense something. They feel threatened. I don't think they know why."

"How is it that you are immune to all of this?"

"I am blessed with the ability to be influential and yet remain non-threatening. They have tried to use their intimidation and coercive tactics against me. I didn't comply. I refused to submit. I demonstrated to them that I was powerful in my own right. I insist on having my own residence, outside of Self Center and the village. This allows me to be physically and socially distant from them.

"I don't question their authority on the island through resistance or non-compliance. I allow them to function as they will. Unless, of course, they go too far. Then, I step in and seek to balance the equation."

"So, you are a mediator of sorts," said N E Wan. "You are the go-between with Self Center and the village. That sounds like it could get complicated."

"I have many sources of information. I also have heightened abilities of observation and intuition," responded A Nic Dotal. "So, I don't let any situation get to the point of crisis. Except once, long ago. I did not realize how far the situation had gone until it was too late. I won't make that mistake again."

With that, A Nic Dotal rose, stepped out of the hut, and proceeded up a trail through the trees. N E Wan, noticing the absence, quickly jumped up and followed.

They walked up and up a trail that ascended the large hill at the center of the island. The trail soon followed a river flowing down the hill. The scenery was breathtaking. The hike was steep, but N E Wan was in such good physical shape, it didn't seem to matter.

They passed close to the base of a giant waterfall. The noise was nearly deafening.

They continued up the trail to the top of the waterfall. It ended at a crystal-clear pond that led right up to the drop-off.

N E Wan stepped into the water. It was cool and refreshing.

"Be very careful," warned A Nic Dotal. "The bottom is extremely slippery. And although it doesn't look like it, there is a swift current. You could easily lose your footing and be swept right over the falls."

At this, N E swam away from the drop-off and into the safer parts of the pond. After cooling off in the refreshing water, N E swam to the shore.

As N E Wan began to climb from the water, A Nic Dotal reached down to assist. When N E accepted the help, a chain swung out from A Nic Dotal's neck, with a key dangling at the end of the chain. A Nic Dotal realized the key was swinging free and immediately pushed it back under A Nic's garment.

The two enjoyed a nice lunch beside the pond. The view from this height was spectacular.

N E spent considerable time looking down on the island, finding the Village of Subjugation, the boats out on the ocean, the beach with the hut, and another beach N E Wan had not seen before.

"What is that beach?" N E asked.

"That beach is near the Lagoon of Lies," replied A Nic Dotal.

"I am not familiar with that lagoon. I thought I had been all around the island on the boats."

"The boats don't go to this lagoon," said A Nic Dotal.

"Why not? It looks beautiful, peaceful. It seems like a wonderful place from up here."

"It is a beautiful and peaceful place. But no one goes there."

"I don't understand," said N E Wan.

"There is an inhabitant who does not permit anyone to come there. This person is a third child of Euphoria and Melancholia. Treachery and deceit surround this person. This is a person feared and avoided by the others on the island, including those at Self Center.

"Should you have the misfortune to come into contact with this person, do your best to excuse yourself and get away. This person is very attractive and can be most charming. However, this person is dangerous. Please remember this. Your friend Viola did not remember and suffered dearly for it."

"What is this person's name?" asked N E Wan.

"This is the youngest child of the two most powerful people on the island and is named B Trayal," replied A Nic Dotal.

"This place gets stranger all this time!" exclaimed N E Wan.

They spent the rest of the day climbing the path above the waterfall to the top of the island. The panoramic view not only gave further perspective on the features and various places on the island, it was also truly magnificent.

Seeing a clearing on the opposite side of the river from Self Center, N E asked, "What is that clearing over there?"

A Nic Dotal replied, "That is my home. We will be going there next."

Following a path across the large hill, they came to another pathway on the other side of the river. This led to the clearing they'd seen from above.

Upon reaching the clearing, N E noticed a well-built home like the ones in Self Center. There was also another structure with many different tools and makeshift machines.

The two entered the first structure. "Welcome to my home," announced A Nic Dotal.

The inside was sparsely decorated. The furniture looked homey and comfortable. It was very clean and tidy.

"This is very nice," said N E Wan. "I like it here. What is the other building?"

"Ah, that is my workshop. Yes, I am an inventor, you see. Many of the machines and tools you use in the village were created by me. I have worked very hard over the years to make life in the village less difficult."

N E walked casually around the workshop, admiring the designs and creativity of the makeshift machines. Toward the back of the workshop, N E Wan saw a table. On the table was a sturdy wooden box with a lock.

Does the key go to that lock? N E wondered.

After they exited the workshop, A Nic Dotal served a delightful dinner. It was nice to listen to the sound of the river, N E thought. *This place is very peaceful and serene.*

Eventually, they descended the hill and returned to the Village of Subjugation. As they entered the village, N E noticed the other villagers staring in wonder and whispering to one another. Then, realizing that none of them had a special relationship with A Nic Dotal, N E Wan realized they were envious. N E hoped this would not be a problem going forward.

A Nic Dotal stepped into N E's hut and asked to see the conch shell again.

A Nic held it up and listened. The voice in the shell said,

"If everyone is right, then no one will be left."

A Nic Dotal smiled, as if recognizing the voice, and then asked, "Is it strange, being a voice in a shell?"

Listening to the shell again, all A Nic Dotal could hear was the sound of the sea.

At this, A Nic Dotal seemed disappointed and bid N E Wan farewell and then stepped out of the hut and walked away.

Feeling content and relaxed, N E sat on the mat and listened to the shell.

"So, you spent the day with A Nic Dotal," said the voice. "That is an influential and powerful friend to have. I imagine the residents of Self Center were getting antsy and worried about you. That would surely get the attention of your friend. Did you have a nice time today?"

"Oh, yes," NE replied. "We went to new places like the waterfall and up to the top of the island."

"The view is so beautiful up there," mused the voice in the shell. "You really get a good perspective of the island from there."

"I thought the same thing. "I was wondering about something A Nic Dotal said concerning the Lagoon of Lies and a person named B Trayal."

"I hope you were warned to stay away from that place and that person," said the voice in the shell, sounding concerned.

"Yes, I was warned, but that was about all," replied N E.

"You should leave it at that."

"I will," promised N E Wan, who then put the shell back into the bag, along with the new shells N E had gathered earlier. Then, N E lay on the mat and fell into a deep sleep.

Chapter 6

N E WAN AROSE the next morning and began the usual routine of washing and eating breakfast. It seemed like a normal morning, until N E Wan noticed the usual morning greetings were not being given to the villagers. At breakfast, even Viola was quiet, not engaging in the usual chatter.

N E leaned toward her and whispered, "What's wrong with everyone?"

"I don't know what you mean," replied Viola, not making eye contact. "Everyone seems fine to me." Then, she rose and walked away from the table.

Fortunately for N E, Vic and Tim Ization were their usual selves, and N E Wan was assigned to the boats on this day. N E worked with them to ready the boats and equipment for the day's harvest.

As N E Wan walked to the beach, ominous clouds were looming in the distance. The water looked dark and menacing.

Tim looked up and announced, "There is a storm coming. Better stay close today. Don't go too far out. You may need to get back in a hurry. I really mean it. This doesn't look good."

Vic said, "Better make sure you have a life vest." Then, he threw N E one of the flotation devices lying on the beach.

N E loaded it into the boat with the rest of the gear and then approached Vic and Tim. "Why is everyone acting so strangely toward me today?"

Tim answered, "Oh, that. Well, only the older people have ever seen A Nic Dotal take a personal interest in a villager. That was a long time ago. So, many of the younger folks, having seen you leave with this powerful and influential person, are envious. You got a day off work. You received special attention from a very special person."

Then Vic chimed in. "They think they deserve a day off and special attention, too. So, they are resentful of you. In a weird way, they think you are getting what was meant for them. Now, in their minds, thanks to you, they are going to be left out. It is really odd, when you think about it. Besides, if A Nic Dotal wanted to spend time with anyone in the village, it would happen, right? But they don't see it that way. People can be funny sometimes."

"What about you two?" asked N E Wan. "Are we okay?"

"Don't worry about us," replied Tim. "We have a very special place in our hearts for A Nic Dotal. We have been through some difficult and painful chapters in our lives.

"We were both physically and emotionally abused by our father, Will B Cruel. No matter what we did, it wasn't good enough. Our father had many troubles in his life. He wasn't a good father or a good person."

"Yes," continued Vic. "We would cry to our mother, but it didn't do any good. She was being abused, as well. Many of the villagers tried to intervene. But he just wouldn't listen. Eventually, they gave up on him.

"One day, he beat our mother to the point of serious injury. That is when A Nic Dotal showed up and confronted him. He tried to threaten A Nic Dotal, but it didn't work. Then, he ran to the beach, ranting and raving like I'd never seen him do before. He took one of the boats and left."

Looking thoughtful and sad, Tim went on. "Wow. I hadn't thought about that for a long time. We were trying to help our mother, but we were too young to really be of any real help. She died that night. I will never forget that.

"The next morning, we spent our time helping to clean up the debris from the storm. Soon, we noticed that one of the boats was gone. Later, we found the boat capsized, floating in the ocean. We never saw our father again. A Nic Dotal visited us on regular basis after that. Eventually, we were able to share our feelings and work through our anger and hurt."

Vic said, "So, N E Wan, we do not have a problem with you spending the day with A Nic Dotal. We will always have a high level of respect for A Nic Dotal. We also like you very much. You work as hard or harder than anyone in the village. You are nice to others, as well."

Tim smiled. "You are just fine with us." Then, looking out to sea, he said, "That storm looks like the one of the worst we've seen. So, be very careful today."

This made N E feel much better. These two friends were special indeed. N E Wan hugged Vic and Tim then pushed one of the boats from the shore and began to paddle.

The waves were choppy and the wind was strong. The boat bobbed up and down, being pushed around. N E kept control of the boat, nonetheless, and started to gather the traps along the edges of the island.

N E Wan returned with the traps and a good harvest of sea creatures. On the beach, other villagers saw the catch and began to smile. They were realizing that N E Wan was still one of them and contributing to the work. N E began to feel a little better.

Then, after lunch, and donning a life vest, N E went out for one last run before the storm overtook the island. As N E paddled in a different direction, the rain and wind buffeted the boat, making it difficult to see. N E retrieved the last trap. But as it was being pulled into the boat, a strong wave hit the side of the boat, tipping it over. N E Wan went face-first into the ocean.

Shocking memories of the earlier shipwreck returned, causing feelings of panic. N E thrashed about as the life vest popped N E Wan to the surface.

The rain was coming down in torrents, and the waves made it difficult to find one's bearings. It was so dark. *Which way was the island?* wondered N E Wan, disoriented and afraid.

Relying on the life vest, N E began kicking and stroking. Soon N E started to feel more and more fatigued. N E's leg brushed against something on the bottom.

The bottom! Keep going! thought N E.

A wave grabbed N E, and soon N E crawled up onto the sandy beach, exhausted.

When N E Wan awoke, N E mused, **This bed is so comfortable**. *I don't want to ever get up. A bed? I don't sleep in a bed? I have a mat on the floor. When was the last time I slept in a bed? Oh, yeah, on the boat. The boat that sank. Speaking of boats, where am I? Where is the boat? What is going on*?

Despite having many questions, N E enjoyed the comfort of the bed for a little longer. Then, getting out of bed, N E noticed that someone had removed N E's wet clothes and put out nice clothes. These were brightly colored clothes. Very comfortable.

Wait! Someone took off my clothes? N E's mind raced.

Then, for the first time since waking, N E Wan looked around the room. It was a nicely appointed bedroom. There was a floor covering and pictures on the walls. Outside the bedroom windows, birds were singing. A beautiful floral bouquet wafted in the air.

N E quietly opened the bedroom door and peeked out.

A voice announced, "Nice to know you are up! Straight ahead is the bathroom. Please make yourself at home."

N E entered the bathroom. It had beautiful towels and soaps. N E Wan washed and performed other morning necessities. Then, N E ventured out to the rest of the house.

Wonderful, familiar smells came from a kitchen area. These smells were familiar, because N E Wan processed these foods in the village. These were fare sent to Self Center. *Self Center*?

"Am I in Self Center?" wondered N E Wan.

Laughing, a voice replied, "Absolutely not! You are in my home. A welcome guest, I might add."

With that, a tall, very attractive person entered the kitchen. An older person from the village was already working in the kitchen.

The stranger said, "If I were to guess, I would venture to say that you are the famous N E Wan. I assume this due to the fact that you were washed up on the beach during a storm. Seems to be becoming a habit."

Putting the pieces together, N E smiled and responded, "This is the Lagoon of Lies, and you are B Trayal."

"Ah, my reputation precedes me," answered B Trayal. "I have not had a guest in a long while, so, let me assure you, this is a treat. But where are my manners? You must be famished!"

With that, B Trayal motioned for N E Wan to be seated at a beautiful table with carved wooden chairs. After N E took one of the comfortable chairs, breakfast was served by the villager on nice, carved plates and ornate bamboo drinking glasses. These place settings were much nicer than anything in the village.

N E Wan was thinking, *B Trayal is charming. Very good looking. Very polite. And, very rich! This is very strange, being served by someone I know from the village.*

Yet being very hungry, N E quickly overcame the discomfort and consumed everything on the plate. Then, N E was given a second helping. B Trayal sat quietly on the other side of the table, watching while leaning back comfortably in a beautiful, carved chair and drinking a strange-looking liquid.

"That does not look like the elixir that A Nic Dotal drinks," said N E Wan, while drinking the same beverage.

"Ah, yes," replied B Trayal. "I had forgotten that A Nic Dotal originally found you and has seemed to adopt you like a puppy. Yes, I see that look of surprise on your face.

"You probably don't realize what a celebrity you have become. Mummy and Daddy seem to be quite obsessed with you. Which, of course, is keeping A Nic Dotal very busy, calming them with assurances of your compliance and good behavior."

"Why are they thinking about me?" asked N E Wan.

Leaning forward and patting N E's hand, B Trayal responded, "Never mind for now. We have plenty of time to talk about whatever is on your mind. As I said, I haven't had a visitor in a long while. I plan to make the most of it. We are going to get to know each other very well."

N E Wan recalled the warning from A Nic Dotal to stay away from B Trayal, but N E didn't seem to have any defenses against this person. This person was very charming and nice to look at. So, N E decided to go along and see what happened.

N E Wan suddenly realized that no one in the village knew what had happened in the storm.

This must have been noticed by B Trayal, who said, "I have my contacts in the village. As you can see, they deliver my supplies and work as my servants. I let them know you are here and that you would probably be staying for a while.

"Of course, I was only guessing as to what you were feeling. I can see by the look on your face that you are comforted by this. Now that you have eaten me out of house and home, we should go for a stroll on the beach."

With that, they both rose. N E Wan started to clean the table.

"Never mind that," B Trayal said. "I have someone who will come in to take care of everything."

N E Wan realized that this someone was the older person from the village. N E was still uncomfortable being served by a fellow villager and felt uneasy. Yet, N E complied and left for the beach.

The Lagoon of Lies was even more beautiful than it appeared from above. Time seemed to stand still while they walked on the smooth sand and looked into the crystal-clear water. B Trayal suggested they remove their clothes and go for a swim.

B Trayal was even better looking undressed. N E Wan must have been staring, because B Trayal laughed with delight.

How can someone be so confident? wondered N E Wan.

With the seduction complete, they swam and played in the water. Then, they made love on the beach. After this, N E Wan felt peaceful and comfortable with B Trayal, any initial discomfort seeming to fade away.

They returned to the home, and N E was given more brightly colored clothing and jewelry to wear. It seemed inappropriate to be wearing these things, but the clothes were so comfortable and nice. The jewelry was even nicer.

It had been a very long while since N E Wan had been so clean, smelled so nice, and looked so good. The admiring look from B Trayal only affirmed this.

As the days passed, walks on the beach continued. The nice home, a nice bed, the sound of birds, and the smell of the flowers seemed like a dream. Enjoying the physical intimacy, the wonderful food, and the mysterious drink was a constant, sensual pleasure.

One evening, after a wonderful day together, B Trayal inquired, "So, tell me your story, N E Wan. I want to know more about you."

N E freely told B Trayal about the father who left and the mother who was ill and passed away. How N E had found out more about N E's missing father in N E's mother's belongings and decided to follow the trail of clues. Making a voyage. The sinking of the ship. Being found on the beach by A Nic Dotal. Life in the village. Friends in the village.

B Trayal sat quietly, seeming to grasp hold of every word, but expressing an unsettled look at the mention of Viola Ated.

Then, feeling accepted and heard, N E Wan began to talk about the inequities between the two groups of people on the island. That it was wrong for one group to dominate and exploit the other. The strange effect the celebrations had on the villagers, and the symbolic differences that reinforced the status of Self Center.

B Trayal seemed enthralled with all that N E Wan said. The feeling of connection and of being understood was intoxicating. Then, they made love in the wonderful bed. N E fell into a blissful slumber.

It was dark when N E was jerked from the bed then dragged from the house and left on a pathway. Stunned and afraid, N E Wan kept asking, "What are you doing? Why are you doing this?"

B Trayal said nothing, just left N E Wan on the path and walked away.

N E sat on the ground for a long time, feeling rejected and hurt. It felt like a punch in the stomach. N E Wan replayed the events of the past several days. The finery. The comfort. The seduction.

N E began to feel very ashamed. Overwhelmed, N E Wan lay back and fell asleep on the path.

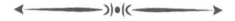

Chapter 7

THE NEXT MORNING, as N E Wan began to climb out of a deep sleep, N E vaguely perceived an all-too-familiar sensation.

Not again, thought N E. *I am being awakened with the poking of a stick.*

"You look awful," came a voice.

N E groggily replied, "Enough with the stick already!"

Laughing, A Nic Dotal helped N E stand-up and stumble to the house by the river. Once there, N E Wan was fed and drank the wonderful elixir.

After N E sat silently for a while, the elixir seemed to provide an unusual, sobering effect. N E Wan soon had a clear head and felt much better, and much worse.

"I'm sorry," N E said with surrender. "I didn't listen. I played the fool. I betrayed my friends. You should be very disappointed in me. You probably hate me."

"That pretty much sums it up," replied A Nic Dotal with a wry smile. "I have prepared a room for you."

With that said, N E Wan was shown to a small, clean, nicely appointed bedroom. On a table in the corner of the room was the bag of shells. N E's clothing from the village had been folded and placed on the bed.

The room was not nearly as chic as the room N E had recently vacated. Nor was the bed as luxurious. However, it felt more like home.

"Thank you," said N E Wan to A Nic Dotal, who stood in the doorway, the key on the neck chain visible.

A Nic Dotal noticed N E staring at it and quickly put it away, out of sight. Then, A Nic Dotal left N E Wan alone in the room.

N E retrieved the conch shell from the bag, lay back on the bed, and listened.

A voice from the shell said, "Well, well, well. You made a fine mess of things, didn't you? I can tell you are already beating yourself up about it, so I will go easy on you."

"I really messed up this time," replied N E Wan. "The funny thing is, I knew where I was, who I was with, and what was happening. Yet, for some stupid reason, I did it anyway. I'm surprised you and A Nic Dotal are still talking to me."

"Yeah, maybe you're right," answered the voice.

At that moment, N E heard nothing more from the shell but the sound of the sea.

N E began to panic. "Hey!" N E exclaimed. "I was just kidding. I didn't really mean it."

"Ha, gotcha!" came the voice with a laugh.

"Great!" said N E Wan, collapsing back on the bed. "I just happen to get a talking shell with a bad sense of humor."

"I like my sense of humor," replied the voice. "I crack myself up. Don't be so hard on yourself. You found out that you are human. Someone discovered your weaknesses and exploited them."

"So, what do I do now?" N E sighed.

"So now, you can have one of several responses to this experience. You can allow yourself to become angry. Your adversary is accustomed to this response and very adept at thwarting any vengeful acts that may ensue. Consequently, you will not benefit, but will be harmed by this response.

"You can become despondent. Blame yourself. Get into a good session of self-loathing. Also harmful to you, and in no way productive or useful.

"Or, you can allow yourself to be humbled by this disaster. Learn from it. Identify the weaknesses that were used against you. Observe and accept more of your real self. Advance your knowledge of human behavior. This is a beneficial and helpful response. It not only gives you insight into other people, but you become more self-aware, and you will be better prepared to handle these situations in the future."

"Huh," replied N E Wan. "That kind of makes sense, I guess. I was beginning to do the second one, and that would have only made matters worse. Just what I need right now, for things to get worse! I need to be much more careful about who I choose to hang around with. I need to surround myself with people who will improve my life, not tear it down."

"My, my," asserted the voice. "That was insightful. I think, maybe, you're getting better already.

"The people you allow into your life will have an impact, big or small, on your quality of life. It is important to really think about what kind of person makes your life better. What are their qualities? How do you feel around them?

"Someone who is untrustworthy, scheming, and manipulative can also be treacherous and downright mean. People who think they have a lot to lose tend to have these characteristics. You just received a large dose of this kind of person.

"B Trayal and those at Self Center think they have a lot to lose. They are anxious that their lifestyle, their status, and their easy way of life will be taken from them. They are protective, suspicious and severe. They will go to great lengths to keep the situation under their control.

"They worry about the people in the village. They know they are outnumbered. They aren't concerned about the villagers' well-being. They are afraid that the villagers will realize they can turn the tables at any moment. Should the people in the village come to understand that they only need to withstand the initial push-back and retaliation from

Self Center to prevail, they would take the upper hand. So, Self Center works hard to keep things status quo.

"Throughout time, for this reason, groups of people have strategically employed various means to give the illusion of superiority above other groups of people. The obvious method has been for one group to physically attack the other. 'To the victor goes the spoils.' The other group is violently beaten into submission. Horrible acts have been enacted by people upon other people.

"But then, after the victory, a problem arises. How do you continue to maintain control? How do you keep the upper hand?

"This has brought on other means of domination, which has included, but not been limited to, establishing a link between the oppressors and divinity. They were 'chosen by God' to lead. Thus, their leadership is legitimate, because it is 'the will of God.'

"Others have chosen bloodlines and lineage to establish their authority. This requires exaltation of an ancestry. Those in charge create a narrative that they are from a long history of noble and powerful rulers. Thus, they are legitimate because of the very blood flowing through their veins.

"This same strategy has sometimes been used by connecting skin pigmentation and other physical characteristics with inherent value and superiority. While these assertions have absolutely no basis in fact, those seeking to keep others subjugated often proclaim that the color of their skin, their physical stature, or other aspects of their appearance make them superior.

"This type of oppression is often enacted through the systemic deprivation of the other group. Those being victimized by this have been deprived of education, denied the ability to engage in the local economy, kept contained in defined communities, denied entrance into social organizations and establishments, and harassed through being labeled inherently criminal or morally inferior."

N E Wan tried to absorb all of this information. N E sat for a while on the bed and then replied, "So, this is a little of what I have seen going on here on the Island of Status Quo. The people at Self Center have established a hierarchy by making themselves seem superior and worthy of their status.

"They live separate from the villagers in nicer homes. They wear the finer clothing and jewelry. They eat the better food. They demand that the villagers work for them and serve them. Then, they present themselves as being beneficent by rewarding the villagers and seeming to acknowledge their efforts.

"They don't, however, encourage the villagers to improve themselves or their situation. The status quo is actually denying the villagers any chance to have a better quality of life. Is this why B Trayal was so interested in my thoughts and opinions about the life here?"

"B Trayal gains influence and social capital by being useful," continued the voice in the shell. "This is why Self Center continues to provide supplies and servants to the Lagoon of Lies. "This chosen life of isolation and luxury would end, if B Trayal was not seen as an asset.

"This is the reason you were drawn in. Finding you on the beach was very fortunate for this purpose. You were essentially delivered to the doorstep. I can only imagine the glee felt, which turned into intense scheming, after you were discovered. B Trayal did not hold you in high esteem. Quite the contrary. You were a means to an end, nothing more."

"I have much to learn," N E said with a sigh. "Why did I succumb to all of the niceties? I simply loved the food, the drink, the bed, smelling good, and not having to go to work! What made me lose all sense of my values?"

The voice replied, "Everyone likes those things. They appeal to the senses. Who doesn't like a comfortable bed? We all like to have choices. We dream of having the luxury and the excesses. You were given the opportunity to relax and be carefree. You didn't have to settle for less. Everything was there for the taking and your enjoyment.

"Unfortunately, all of that came at the expense of other people. People you care about. People who are being deprived of this lifestyle, while working to provide it to others.

"It was also an illusion. None of that was free. You paid a price. You told them about your real position and your reaction to the systems on the Island of Status Quo. This was the information B Trayal needed to satisfy Self Center. You were betrayed, and for that you may end up paying a heavy price.

"You are safe, for now. A Nic Dotal will protect you from harm. However, there will come a time when that protection will not hold. Then, you will answer to them. So, for now, reflect on what you have learned. Glean all you can from A Nic Dotal's wealth of wisdom."

Feeling overwhelmed, N E Wan placed the shell back in the bag and wept.

The remainder of the day was quiet. A Nic Dotal came into the bedroom and explained that several errands needed to be done, so N E would be alone for most of the day. N E was instructed to stay in and around the house. Not to wander. Then, in the morning, they would do the errands together.

N E Wan spent the day exploring the house and sitting by the river. The water was swift and deep. The sound of the waterfall was peaceful. The world here felt safe, but outside seemed much more dangerous. Yet, this realization did not produce fear.

This was surprising. Seeing the world more clearly resulted in a strange sense of empowerment.

Learning to better play the game gave N E a sense of confidence and resolve.

A Nic Dotal returned that evening, and they shared a quiet meal together. N E Wan was not surprised that A Nic Dotal ate the same food as the villagers and wore similar clothing. N E did not miss the finer food or the nice clothes and jewelry. N E Wan did, however, miss the soft mattress and smelling nice.

N E walked around the grounds after dinner, thinking. N E noticed the workshop and decided to go in to look at all the handmade tools and gadgets. There, N E noticed that box again. The locked box.

What was in it? Was the key to the box on the chain around the neck of A Nic Dotal?

That would need to wait for another day, N E decided. N E Wan bid A Nic Dotal good night, went to bed, and fell asleep.

Chapter 8

ONE OF THE ERRANDS that A Nic Dotal had to run on the day of N E Wan's return was to Self Center. B Trayal had deposited N E on the path and already left the Lagoon of Lies to report on N E's subversive intentions. Thus, A Nic Dotal had been summoned to Self Center, to make a report.

A Nic Dotal had long been the go-between for Self Center and the Village of Subjugation. Having succeed in arbitrating several issues and disputes over the years, those at Self Center had ensured that A Nic Dotal could live near the river, outside of Self Center and unmolested. So, in order to maintain this situation, A Nic Dotal needed to answer when called.

A Nic Dotal entered Self Center and noticed that the inhabitants had already gathered and were waiting to be addressed. Chairs had been arranged in the courtyard. Two large chairs were arranged at the front, with Euphoria and Melancholia seated in them. Four other, smaller chairs faced them. These chairs contained Art Official, Sue Perior, Mister Ection, and Miss Demeanour.

A Nic Dotal was accustomed to standing, without a chair, in a place facing the two large chairs and the audience. After taking the assigned place, A Nic Dotal immediately noticed the look of displeasure on all of the faces. This meeting would require significant powers of persuasion.

Melancholia began the meeting. "We have an imminent threat that needs to be addressed, and addressed severely." As the others assented, Melancholia continued, "We have been informed, A Nic Dotal, that your newest little interest is causing problems and has made overtures against us. This little project of yours has lofty personal aspirations that are not in the interest of the status quo."

Sue Perior chimed in, "This N E Wan has won the hearts of many villagers. They feel a strong connection, maybe even loyalty."

Art Official interrupted. "Well, maybe that was the case. Now that fate has delivered N E Wan to the influence and guiles of B Trayal, the villagers don't feel the same anymore. They feel, well, betrayed."

Miss Demeanour responded, "This N E Wan cannot be allowed back in the village at any cost."

"Not only that, we must insist on an inquisition," snarled Mister Ection. "This must be put to rest once and for all. It cannot be allowed to fester."

As they all mumbled their approval at these comments, Euphoria proclaimed, "Hear, hear! This all sounds so dire. We all know that B Trayal tends to exaggerate. Maybe this hasn't yet reached the crisis point. We did call A Nic Dotal here today. Let's hear the report."

A Nic Dotal had been standing quietly on the assigned spot, without a chair, listening. Then, after a moment of theatrical pause, A Nic replied, "Thank you for inviting me here today. As you are well aware, I have been actively involved with this situation since the arrival of N E Wan.

"We share in the desire to make sure things on the island do not get out of hand. For this very purpose, Art, Sue and myself have been involved in making sure this person was quickly assimilated into the village. "It is, in fact, largely due to the influence and cooperation of Art and Sue that this has been successful for so long."

As A Nic Dotal said this, Art and Sue smiled and seemed very pleased with themselves. Euphoria was also smiling at them and nodding. The other members were not smiling and did not look pleased in the least.

Melancholia replied, "Art and Sue have done a reasonable job with the villagers all these years. They also have managed this new situation, up to this point. However, regardless of what seemed to be assimilation, the reality is that this N E Wan has been observing us the entire time, in order to find our weaknesses. This is being done in hopes of making a move against us.

"B Trayal does exaggerate and does have ulterior motives. Nonetheless, this news is disturbing and cannot be ignored."

Art and Sue slumped into their chairs at this. Euphoria still seemed to be smiling and quite content. The others were expressing their agreement with Melancholia.

Quickly responding, A Nic Dotal said, "Yes, Melancholia, I agree. This does bring to light serious new information. For this very reason, I immediately intervened in this situation and have brought N E Wan to my home. This way, any influence on the villagers is kept at bay.

"This also gives me time to assess the situation with the villagers and with N E Wan. I assure you that N E Wan has been compliant and cooperative with this new arrangement. Going forward, I will conduct supervised visits with N E Wan, when going to the village, thus making sure no untoward actions occur."

Sue and Art began smiling again. Euphoria was still smiling. The others looked less angry but still skeptical.

Melancholia spoke. "As you wish, A Nic Dotal. You usually do as you say. We will allow this for now. However, we will still hold our court with this N E Wan in the near future. You will deliver this person to us at that time."

Relieved that the crisis had been avoided, A Nic Dotal replied, "You are more than fair. And yes, I will follow through with my continued supervision and involvement."

At that, the meeting was adjourned, and the people dispersed. Servants removed the chairs and worked to return the courtyard to its usual beauty.

A Nic Dotal quickly exited Self Center in an effort to avoid further contact, especially with Mister Ection and Miss Demeanour. They were continually watching and waiting for A Nic Dotal to slip up in some way, so they could eliminate this special status that A Nic Dotal enjoyed.

As A Nic Dotal walked down the path, weighed down heavily by thoughts of a past and heartbreaking failure. *It cannot play out that way again,* thought A Nic Dotal. *I must find a way to make it different this time.*

N E Wan's feelings and observations are accurate. They are also dangerous. And what's going on with that shell? Why doesn't it talk to me? What does the shell talk about with N E Wan?

With questions swirling around within, A Nic Dotal slowly began to hatch a plan. A plan that will reconnect N E Wan with the villagers, somehow keep Self Center at bay, and also give N E Wan a new revelation about the history of the Island of Status Quo.

Deep in thought, A Nic Dotal looked up and realized that the path had come to an end. Entering the house, A Nic Dotal found N E Wan seated at a table, looking at shells.

Since that day was coming to a close, A Nic Dotal prepared the evening meal.

Chapter 9

THE NEXT MORNING, A Nic Dotal informed N E Wan that they would be spending the day together. N E seemed pleased with this idea, to get out and walk around again.

"Our first stop will be the Village of Subjugation," announced A Nic Dotal.

N E froze and then stared in disbelief at A Nic Dotal.

"The members of Self Center are very suspicious of you right now," said A Nic Dotal. "We need to move quickly to allay these fears. Therefore, it is imperative we go to the village."

"I thought you liked me," said N E Wan with a wry smile. "Now you want to throw me to the wolves?"

Smiling, A Nic Dotal replied, "Now I do feel betrayed."

N E Wan was oddly comforted by having A Nic Dotal make light of such a serious situation.

The two left the house and proceeded down the path to the village. Near the entrance to the village, Mister Ection and Miss Demeanour were relaxing near the trees. They were lounging in comfortable chairs, while servants held umbrellas above them for shade. As the two walked by, nothing was said.

Just inside the entrance to the village, Art and Sue were waiting.

"Nice to see you, A Nic Dotal," greeted Sue. Art just smiled and nodded.

"Thank you," replied A Nic Dotal. "We are on our way to see the village."

A Nic Dotal and N E Wan walked into the center of the village. Many villagers were just sitting down to breakfast. The hum of conversation, which was evident before they entered, came to a halt. Every villager sat quietly and stared at N E Wan.

"N E Wan, come sit with us!" shouted Vic and Tim.

Relieved, N E took leave of A Nic Dotal and went to sit with Vic and Tim.

"I'll just be a moment," said A Nic Dotal, walking over to a group of older villagers and leaving N E Wan to sit.

"So, how was it?" asked Vic.

"I bet it was super-nice," said Tim.

"It was wonderful and nice," admitted N E Wan. "But I really shouldn't be talking about it. Besides, I got thrown out on my ear."

"No way!" exclaimed Tim.

"You got tossed? Sounds familiar." Vic sighed and looked at Viola.

"I was completely humiliated, okay?" N E sighed. "I made a complete fool of myself. I know it.

So, go ahead and rub it in. I was an idiot and got what I deserved."

At this point, N E Wan realized that no one else was talking. Their voices were carrying because of the silence. N E Wan looked around and saw all the villagers staring. A couple of people were whispering, while some villagers were actually smiling.

Then, Viola rose from a different table, walked over, and gave N E Wan a hug. "Welcome home. We missed you."

"The only thing we missed was that we had to do the extra work!" yelled Tim.

The villagers laughed at this. Then, the conversation began to hum again.

N E Wan spent the remainder of breakfast time catching up with Viola, all the while thinking, *How could everyone be so forgiving? Why are they taking me back? I betrayed them. I let them down.*

Soon, N E Wan was assigned work on the boats, and N E departed for the beach. It was strange to feel so warm and happy to be back at work. This was home. These people were the next best thing to family.

"Don't worry," announced Vic. "We got your boat back."

"You owe us a life vest, though," added Tim. "No, really. You do."

"I will make it up to you," replied N E Wan.

The banter went back and forth for a while. Then, it was time to get to work.

N E started rowing the boat out into the water and quickly became fatigued. How long had it been? *I feel so out of shape*, N E thought. *This is going to be a rough few days. All that lazing around is going to cost me all right.*

Each night, N E returned to the home of A Nic Dotal. For the first few days, the villagers gave them strange looks. After that, they simply went about their business.

A Nic Dotal and N E Wan spent a lot of time talking about the day's experiences and other questions N E had. N E Wan was able to be in the village every day and then leave to spend special time with A Nic Dotal. This was the best of both worlds, and N E Wan was going to make the most of it.

Sooner than expected, N E returned to form and was easily able to perform the duties assigned. Art and Sue still appeared in the distance during each day. Mister Ection and Miss Demeanour were not seen again, although N E suspected they were out there somewhere. Watching and waiting.

One evening, after a nice meal and lively conversation, N E Wan entered the bedroom. The bag of shells was on the table.

I haven't spoken to the voice in the shell for a while, N E thought.

Picking up the bag and turning to the bed, N E saw a strange sight.

Can this be? Then, N E Wan put down the bag, reached over, and picked up the chain with the key.

N E Wan's heart began pounding. Picking up the key, N E Wan called for A Nic Dotal. There was no answer. A Nic Dotal was nowhere to be found.

N E went to the box in the workroom, inserted the key into the lock, and turned it. Then, N E lifted the heavy wooden lid and looked inside. It was a book.

N E lifted the book from the box. It had a thick, heavy binding.

N E opened to the book to the first page and read:

A Story of Avery Wan
By A Nic Dotal

N E Wan's hands began to shake. The book made a heavy thud as it dropped to the floor.

Chapter 10

THOUGHTS AND EMOTIONS began to overwhelm N E. There, on the floor, was a book, written by A Nic Dotal, about Avery Wan, N E Wan's father. The father who had abandoned the family. The father who left on a journey and never returned.

This is the story of my father, thought N E Wan, nudging the book with a foot. *My father knew A Nic Dotal. A Nic Dotal knew my father. Did my father live on the Island of Status Quo? Is that where they met?*

N E picked up the book and, going to a nearby table, set it down. Then, N E went to the house, picked up the bag of shells, and removed the conch shell. N E Wan asked, "Are you my father?"

The voice in the shell answered, "Yes."

"Are you dead?"

"I think so."

"How did you get into this shell?"

"I don't know."

"I have so many questions."

"I am sure you do. First, read the book. Then we will talk."

"Do you… Did you love me and my mother?"

"Yes, very much. I still do."

"Did you know she is dead?"

"No, I didn't."

"She is."

"N E Wan, I am so sorry. This makes me very sad."

"Me, too. I will read the book, then we will talk."

"That sounds good to me."

With that, N E Wan replaced the conch shell in the bag of shells, returned to the workshop, picked up the book, and sat down at the table to read.

A Story of Avery Wan

By A Nic Dotal

"You're pregnant!" shouted Avery Wan. "We must celebrate. This is wonderful news."

From this moment on, Avery Wan doted over the mother of his child. He provided for her every need. She was often ill and could not work. He became very serious about their future and their finances. He took on extra work at the docks near their home.

He tried to support his wife and their new baby, but this proved to be more and more challenging. The extra work was welcomed, however it didn't generate enough money and it took precious time from his new family.

In the beginning, the birth seemed like an event that would happen far into the future. There would be plenty of time to save up enough money to support the family.

Then, in what seemed like a flash, the day arrived. A child was born. Avery held the child in his arms. A deep feeling of love engulfed him. He also felt a tremendous weight of responsibility.

Soon, the child was home. They were such a happy family. They laughed and played, and their life together was wonderful.

Yet, with a new baby and a wife who suffered from illness, Avery was compelled to work long hours. One evening, his wife told him she was worried about him. He was working so hard and so long, it was wearing him down.

Avery then broke down and explained their finances. Their meager savings would not support them. He wept and confessed his fears and feelings of hopelessness.

His wife replied, "Something will happen that will change everything. You will see."

Avery didn't derive much comfort from this. He also didn't have a solution to their situation.

Working the various jobs on the docks, he came into contact with many types of people. Some were local and familiar. Others came and went on the boats that arrived and departed each day. These others spoke in strange languages. They had different customs and sang songs from distant lands. Some liked to tell stories.

One of these storytellers was particularly interesting. While he worked, Avery liked to listen as those stories were told.

One evening, after a small group had gathered, a stranger told an unusual story. This story was about a distant land, a strange and different land. The people from this place produced rare spices.

These spices were greatly desired and often sold at very high prices.

The small crowd was enraptured as the story was told. Avery, on the other hand, thought he saw an opportunity.

After the crowd had dispersed, Avery went to the storyteller and asked if the story was true.

The storyteller became very serious. In a low voice, the storyteller said, "Yes, my friend, the story is true. In fact, in two weeks' time, a boat will be departing from this very dock and sailing to this land. Once there, this boat will be loaded with these spices. Then, the boat and its crew will deliver these spices to a very wealthy buyer.

"Let me tell you, whoever is working on this boat will be well paid. If you choose to come, we will save a place for you. I have seen you. You work hard, and you know what you are doing. I assure you, on this one voyage you will make more money than you will make working all your jobs on the docks combined."

Immediately, Avery replied, "Save me a place on the boat. I will go with you."

The storyteller smiled. "Yes, my friend. You will be a welcome addition to my crew."

For the first time in so many months, Avery Wan felt hopeful. He hurried home and told his wife about the storyteller and the good fortune to be had. They discussed the time the voyage would take. Avery lamented all the time he would be away from his wife and child. Yet, they decided this would be the best chance they would ever have.

Over the next week, Avery continued to work hard on the docks. The storyteller, really the captain, gathered the crew together. The duties were assigned, the route explained, and payment finalized. Avery was happy with his duties on the boat. He understood the route that would be taken, and he was overjoyed at the payment he would receive.

As the departure grew near, Avery explained the voyage to his wife, gathered his belongings for safekeeping, and spent special time with her and their child. He wanted to remember everything about them, while he was at sea.

The day came. Tearful goodbyes were made. Avery lifted the cloth bag with his belongings onto his back and walked to the boat.

Avery boarded the craft and was shown to the crew quarters. Hammocks were affixed to strong poles, three high. Avery chose the top one and tossed his bag onto the hammock.

His first assignment was in the galley. He worked peeling and chopping, helping to make the meal for the guests on the boat. From the galley, he was not privy to the boarding of the passengers. Nor to the commotion on deck, as they prepared to get underway. He did, however, feel the sensation of the boat moving away from the dock and out to sea.

Soon, the meal had been prepared. It smelled wonderful. Avery was allowed to sample the food as it was being cooked. It also tasted wonderful.

He inquired of the cook, "Do you always have such fine cuisine on all your voyages?"

"Heavens no," the cook replied. "This is a special trip, you see, lad. Do you know who is out there in the dining hall as we speak? It is only the family that owns this boat and many others like it. Very hoity-toity. Yes, we have in our midst the one and only royal family of the sea."

"They sound very important," said Avery Wan.

"They are very rich, that's true." The cook laughed. "And they think they are very important. Turns out, they ain't no different than you and me."

The cook opened the galley door a crack and looked into the dining area with Avery Wan.

"Ya see the captain over there?" said the cook, pointing at a large table in the middle of the dining hall.

Avery looked through the opening and saw the familiar face of the captain sitting at the head of the large table. "Who are the people sitting at the captain's table?"

"Hmmm," said the cook. "I think that person sitting to the captain's right is A Nic Dotal. Very nice person. Doesn't seem to take on airs like the rest of 'em. To the left of the captain is a couple who works for the company. Real high up in the company, that is. They are Art Official and Sue Perior. They really seem to take themselves seriously, if ya know what I mean."

"I don't see the so-called royal family," replied Avery.

"Ah, let me see. There they are. They brought their own table with them, since this is a special voyage. They also brought their three brats. I don't like those kids one bit.

"See the couple? They are called Euphoria and Melancholia. They are a pair of strange birds. Ya know, people who think they're better than you and me, for no reason. That's them. Then there's the three kids. The first two go by Mister and Miss, and the littlest one is B Trayal. Keep your distance from them youngens. I mean it."

With that, they went back to work, putting away the stores and cleaning the galley. After work, Avery was making his way back to his quarters when he was pushed from behind and knocked into a wall.

After the initial shock, he noticed one of the children running to the railing and throwing up. Remembering what the cook had said, Avery kept his distance and continued to his quarters, where he went to sleep.

The next morning, after breakfast, Avery was assigned to mop the deck. This was greatly needed, due to the amount of vomit splattered on and around it. Although the smell was gagging and the sight was worse, he had to smile. He imagined the entire royal family puking over and on and around the railing throughout the evening.

He thought, "People are people. No one is better than anyone else. So, why bother putting on airs and acting like that?"

Then, as if on cue, the stateroom door burst open, and Melancholia came stumbling out, shouting back into the room, "This is ridiculous! We have been throwing up everything we ate last night. We haven't gotten any sleep. How can you even think of breakfast?"

Coming through the door with the three children, Euphoria replied, "My dear, I found the evening fare to be absolutely delicious. Why, I even gave my compliments to the cook. I can't imagine why you insisted on vomiting all night. I slept like a baby."

Euphoria smiled at Avery Wan then proceeded with the green-faced family down the deck to the dining hall. Avery stood, leaning on the railing and looking in their direction, until they had disappeared. Then, he looked out over the sea. In the distance was an ominous bank of very dark clouds. He could see the lightning from the storm and hear the rumble of the thunder.

"Looks bad." Avery turned to see the captain standing nearby, looking at the clouds. "Looks like we are in for a bit of trouble. You still remember how to deploy and man the lifeboats, don't ya boy?"

"Yes, Captain," replied Avery. "We repeated the drill several times before we left."

"Hope you won't need to do it," said the captain, sounding worried. "But I'd certainly be ready."

Avery took another look at the oncoming storm, and then packed up the mop and bucket and left the deck. He proceeded to the galley.

As he pushed the door open, a voice said, "Ouch." Looking around the door, he saw that he had hit A Nic Dotal with the door.

"I am so sorry!" he exclaimed.

"Not your fault, actually," replied A Nic Dotal. "I was reading this map and not watching where I was going. My name is A Nic Dotal. And you are?"

"My name is Avery Wan," he answered. "Again, I am very sorry to have hit you with the door."

"Please, please," repeated A Nic Dotal. "It was completely my fault. And it is very nice to meet you, Mr. Wan. Now, I bid you good day."

Then, A Nic Dotal walked away.

"Not what I expected," thought Avery. "This one seems like a regular person. Very polite, as well."

Avery chopped and peeled in the galley, getting ready for the lunch meal. "I hear you received a compliment from one of the royal family," he said to the cook.

"Why yes, I did," the cook replied. "Sometimes, it is nice to be appreciated."

As they prepared the meal, the boat began to rock to and fro. This proved challenging, with all the pots and pans sliding about.

"Feels like a gale," said the cook.

"I was looking at the clouds earlier," said Avery. "They were very dark and worrisome."

The wind began to grow stronger. The waves buffeted the boat. The royal family began to puke again. Then, a large wave washed over the deck. The boat began taking on water and listing to the side. A bell began to sound. "Abandon Ship!" was heard throughout the vessel.

Avery hurriedly donned foul-weather gear and a life vest. Then, he proceeded to the lifeboats. "Where was the captain? Where was the rest of the crew?" he wondered, as he readied each craft.

When the boats were ready, the passengers were on deck. They looked very worried. Each had a life vest but didn't seem to have rain gear.

Avery helped A Nic Dotal, Art Official, and Sue Perior into one of the boats. He yelled above the wind, "The rest of the crew is not here. Do any of you know how to handle a craft like this?"

Art and Sue looked terrified as they shook their heads. Avery wondered why these people who worked for a company that owns boats didn't know anything about boats.

A Nic Dotal shouted, "I am proficient with many seafaring crafts. We will be okay here! Please, see to the family, and make sure that they are safe."

Avery lowered the lifeboat into the water. Then, he turned and assisted the children and parents into a second boat. Still seeing no one else, he climbed into the lifeboat then lowered the craft into the water.

The waves were high, and the boat was bouncing around. The family huddled in a corner of the boat. Avery quickly rowed away from the larger ship. As they looked back, the ship was on its side and mostly under water.

Avery continued to row, staying close to the other lifeboat. Water was collecting on the floor of the boat. Avery asked the passengers to start bailing it out. No one moved. So, Avery spent part of his time bailing and the other part rowing. No one else seemed to want to help. Even if it was to save their own lives.

Soon, the wind died down and the waves began to calm. A Nic Dotal called from the other boat, "Mr. Wan, is it? Thank you for saving our lives. We are wet and tired. Why don't we rest for a time? Then we can figure out our next moves."

Avery placed the oars in the boat, lay back, and fell asleep.

"What is that?" wondered Avery, coming out a deep sleep.

Opening one eye, he saw the sun was shining, and a child was poking him with an oar.

"He looks alive," said the child.

Avery sat up and looked around. The people in his boat were staring at him, and the people in the other boat were staring at him.

"Nice to have you back with us, Mr. Wan," said A Nic Dotal. "The good news is, I think I know where we are. The other good news is, these boats are stocked with food and water. They also have a nice covering to protect us from the sun."

"What's the bad news?" asked Melancholia.

"The bad news is that we seem to be the only survivors, and we are out in the middle of the ocean," answered Sue.

"Brilliant deduction," sneered Melancholia. "If you know where we are, then you should know which direction we need to go."

"Right you are," A Nic Dotal said with a smile. "Simply follow me. If I remember the map correctly, there should be land in this direction."

With that, A Nic Dotal began rowing away. Avery quickly grabbed the oars and followed. They spent the remainder of the day rowing and resting. The weather cooperated, and they made good progress.

The sun set, and they rowed in the dark for a long while. Then, Sue Perior asked, "What's that?"

Avery began to scan the horizon. It was dark, as there was very little moonlight. Then, he saw it. Small dots of flickering lights. He and A Nic Dotal began to row toward the lights.

As dawn approached, they were able to make out what looked like an island. Soon, they were in the shallow water. Then, they pulled the boats onto the beach.

They stumbled out of the boats and lay on the beach. Their faces looked relieved, while some wept. Then, they gathered themselves together, and Melancholia began to give orders.

Interrupting and pointing toward the tree line, one of the children yelled, "Look!"

The group turned to look and saw a line of people standing near the trees. A Nic Dotal stepped forward and began to speak.

"Hello. Our boat sank in the storm. We made it to this island on these lifeboats. Would you be willing to aid us in our time of need?"

One of the islanders replied, "Yes, we will help you. Come with us."

The castaways were led through the trees, along a path, to an opening. There were crudely built huts scattered around the area. People were tending fires at each hut.

They were led to a three-sided stand made from bamboo and palm fronds. "You may stay here for now," said the guide.

Melancholia said, "Here? This? You can't be serious!"

Euphoria replied, "How quaint. You have to admit, this is better than sleeping on a boat. It could be fun."

A Nic Dotal thanked the islander, and the group began to settle in.

For the next several days, islanders brought food and water to the group. A Nic Dotal spoke often with the island people and learned much about their ways. Avery Wan assisted the islanders in gathering food and water. The others simply watched and complained.

One evening, after a simple meal, Melancholia and Euphoria called a meeting with Art Official and Sue Perior.

Melancholia began, "We are not leaving here any time soon. There is obviously no one looking for us. We need to make a plan to start taking over around here."

Euphoria said, "The islanders are a delightful group. They smile and seem quite happy. However, they are not organized, nor are they efficient."

"Yes," added Art. "They gather, instead of planting and growing their food."

"You are correct, Art." smiled Euphoria. "They should plant, and they should make better use of the sea. Our lifeboats are better than their makeshift canoes. We will help them build boats, clear the trees, and plant fruits and vegetables."

"Even their homes are scattered about," added Sue Perior. "We will put them to work and make this into an organized village."

"Sounds like we have the beginnings of a plan," concluded Melancholia. "We will have them shaped up in no time."

Over the next few months, Euphoria enlisted the help of Avery Wan to design and build boats. A Nic Dotal gathered those who knew the most about the island flora, and they began to identify the various plants, discover their nutritional value and medicinal qualities, and select those used for clothing. Melancholia directed Art and Sue on better building methods and insisted they get the islanders to work.

Soon, the trees had been cleared, and crops were planted and growing. Several boats were seaworthy. Traps and nets were assembled, and a sea harvest was coming in each day. The islanders constructed many new bamboo huts that were sturdier and more waterproof than the ones before.

The huts were built around a large, open area. Tables were constructed, chairs were crafted, and poles were anchored in the ground to support palm frond roofs. Art and Sue explained to the islanders that this is where they would process the food and make clothing.

One evening, Avery Wan pulled A Nic Dotal aside. "The islanders are very pleased with the improvements we have helped them make. They are working very hard each day to make this happen. They are also beginning to ask why several people in the group don't seem to do any work."

A Nic Dotal replied, "Yes, I see. I have noticed the same thing myself. I was partly thinking they would eventually join in and start to help out. Then, I started to notice that they don't think they need to work, since they are the ones who made all this happen in the first place. It seems I will need to speak with them soon."

The next morning, A Nic Dotal asked to speak with Euphoria and Melancholia.

"What is it, A Nic Dotal?" demanded Melancholia.

A Nic Dotal began, "There is no doubt that the influence we have made here is beneficial to the islanders and to the rest of us, as well. The ideas, the planning, and the implementation have proceeded nicely. Yet, some are questioning why your group does not do any of the actual work."

"What ingratitude!" scoffed Melancholia. "They are happy and should be happy that we came along. We are the reason this place has been cleaned up and put into running order. They are eating better and more than when we came. Their roofs don't leak. They should be doing anything but complaining."

"Do you think there will be a problem?" asked Euphoria, smiling.

"I hope not," replied A Nic Dotal. "I will continue to monitor the situation."

As A Nic Dotal was walking away, Avery came up and asked, "Well, how did it go?"

A Nic Dotal relayed the gist of the conversation.

Avery exclaimed, "What? We did the work! We made all of this happen. Sure, they had some good ideas and organizational skills, but that doesn't compare to what all the rest of us did."

"Yes, I understand this," said A Nic Dotal. "You are accurate in your observations. However, I have encountered people who believe and behave like this before. They can be formidable, even dangerous."

After the meeting with A Nic Dotal, Melancholia called a meeting with Euphoria, Art, Sue, and even the children.

"Listen to me and listen good. If we don't get a handle on this situation, it will spin out of our control. We need to get as many islanders on our side as we can. We need to do this now.

"Identify anyone who is impressionable and anyone who seems influential. This includes the children. If anyone in this bunch starts turning the people against us, we will have to go to great measures to regain control. It is far more effective to have them turn on one another, if need be."

"So, what are we supposed to do exactly?" asked B Trayal.

Art replied, "Well, this is my specialty. First, you observe them at their work, and you go to their homes. Look for anything worthy of praise. Tell them how impressed you are. Be specific as to what you admire. Then, you will see them smile. Most people are suckers for genuine praise. So, make sure you really mean it.

"Now, once you have 'buttered them up,' you ask them what they think about all of the improvements in the village. What's their favorite food? Help them to recognize the positive growth that has occurred. Then, slowly bring up all the contributions our group has made. Finally, tell them how much they have to be thankful for."

"Wow, I can do that!" said B Trayal smiling.

The entire group was smiling. Even Melancholia had a bit of smile. Euphoria said, "Looks like we have a plan. Let's all get to work— Oops! Pun intended!"

A Nic Dotal observed as the group began to be more social and involved with the islanders. It was strange to watch them be friendly and amiable. A Nic Dotal realized what they were doing and then thought, "Was one to admire them or be horrified?"

Avery Wan spoke continually with A Nic Dotal about the group and his disapproval of them. "They aren't any better than any of the rest of us," he often said. "They need to carry their weight. This cannot be tolerated."

A Nic Dotal told Avery to be very careful about these views. Yet, Avery started to speak with some of the villagers anyway.

Also during this time, A Nic Dotal acquired a stick. This was a common-looking stick. It was also a formidable weapon. A Nic Dotal practiced with the stick regularly. The group, along with the villagers, began to take notice.

Art and Sue exerted more control over the village. They named it the Village of Subjugation and had an entrance constructed to the village. They began to assign the villagers to their tasks and duties. They also instituted a start and stop signal for work each day.

Then, they announced that, in three days' time, there would be a celebration. All would get a day off of work, and awards would be given.

Many of the villagers became excited by this. Others seemed to show skepticism. This negative reaction was observed by Sue, and plans were made to bring the others on board.

By this time, Art Official's guidance had been carried out successfully. Connections had been made. Many of the villagers had been won over. Mister Ection, Miss Demeanour, and B Trayal had a steady stream of information coming from the children regarding their parents.

The group now had a good idea of who would potentially pose a problem. They also had information on Avery Wan.

The adults and the children stepped up their campaign to win over those who had been singled out. Their efforts were quite successful. Euphoria selected Avery and started to pay more attention to him.

"You are such a positive asset here in the village," beamed Euphoria. "I so enjoyed the time I worked with you on the boats. You are quite skilled and inventive."

Avery felt conflicted. It was nice to hear the compliments, and they seem to be from the heart. But the realization that these people were exploiting the villagers still burned in his mind.

The Day of Celebration arrived. The villagers had been preparing a feast for several days, so they all could have this day off. They were allowed to sleep in. The group mingled with the villagers, and everyone was smiling.

Then, the time came for the awards. All of the awards were connected to the work. After the awards came an announcement.

Art Official began, "This is such a glorious and momentous occasion. So many of our best workers have been recognized and awarded. Now, I have an even greater announcement to make. We have identified the best builders in the village. We want to award you by allowing you to build our new homes. We will be moving to a place we will call Self Center. We will also now call this the Island of Status Quo."

The members of the group were positioned around the villagers and began to applaud. The villagers joined in. Then, the celebration ended, and everyone was dismissed.

While they were dispersing, a noise rose from one of the huts. It was the home of the Ization family. The father had long been known to lose his temper, sometimes becoming violent. The villagers tried to intervene, but he was larger than most, and they had to back off.

This time sounded louder and more violent than ever before. As the people stood outside the hut, a figure pushed through them. It was A Nic Dotal.

A Nic Dotal burst into the hut, grabbed the father, and dragged him out in front of the people. The father came at A Nic Dotal, who started whirling the stick, hitting him again and again. Then, A Nic Dotal began to lunge with the stick, striking the father in the stomach.

The father, bloodied and screaming with rage, ran off toward the beach. A Nic Dotal instructed the villagers to attend to the family. The mother died that evening. The boys went to live with relatives in the village.

To anyone who was noticing, another strange event happened after that night. Euphoria, Melancholia, Art, Sue, the children, and even B Trayal looked at A Nic Dotal with a new respect and admiration.

The days passed. Life in the village became routine. Self Center was quickly built on a flat section of a hill that rose in the center of the island. This was near a large pool that fed a roaring waterfall. Everyone quickly learned to be cautious when swimming in the pool. The bottom was slippery, and the swift current would sweep someone over the falls, if they were not careful.

The homes in Self Center were nicer and more spacious than the ones in the village. Art and Sue began to have the older people in the village work as servants at Self Center. They also started to have the best food and nicest clothing sent out of the village and up the hill, to Self Center.

A Nic Dotal also left the village and built a home near the river that ran down a steep hill in the center of the island.

Avery Wan was not invited to Self Center and remained in the village. He continued to work hard and do his part. Yet, he still burned with indignation toward those who lived in Self Center. He would sometimes sit up at night with a few of the villagers and express his views. Most of the time, the villagers would just sit and listen.

A Nic Dotal would work on new tools and other items to help the villagers. A Nic made visits to the village and to Self Center, checking in on Vic and Tim. Both the groups in the village and in Self Center came to rely on the wisdom and skills of arbitration A Nic Dotal possessed.

One evening, as A Nic Dotal was leaving Self Center, Melancholia approached. "We are becoming concerned with Avery Wan. He is continuing to stir up dissent in the village. He respects you and may listen to you."

"I will see what I can do," replied A Nic Dotal then bid Melancholia farewell and went to the house by the river.

Struggling with this situation, A Nic Dotal thought, "What am I to do? I agree with Avery Wan. He is a good man and is only thinking about the welfare of the villagers. Yet, I am also concerned with his safety. I fear the punishment from Self Center will be severe. But, how can I ask him to stop doing what he thinks is right?"

The next day, A Nic Dotal visited Avery Wan. "You are doing what you think is right. You see what is happening here. You know that the villagers are being exploited. I cannot advise you to be silent. I can advise you to be careful. You are endangering yourself and anyone who shares these views."

Avery Wan thanked A Nic Dotal and promised he would try to be more careful.

Avery trusted the villagers who shared his views. They would speak together often. They were becoming emboldened. They began to make a plan that would change the dynamic and bring down Self Center. What Avery did not know was that these villagers also spoke of these feelings at home. Their children listened to their discussions. Children being children, they talked to their friends, not understanding the gravity of the situation.

One evening after the meal, Art and Sue came to the village with B Trayal. Art called the villagers into the square. After they were assembled, B Trayal went from person to person, eventually pointing out five people. These people were then led out of the village, and the other villagers were dismissed. One of those chosen was Avery Wan.

The villagers were marched to Self Center. As they entered, they noticed a grouping with Euphoria, Melancholia, Sue Perior, and soon, Art Official seated in chairs. The villagers stood before them.

Melancholia rose and spoke. "You are hereby being charged with sedition and treason. You have actively been engaged in undermining the fabric of our society. You have actively been engaging in plans to overthrow Self Center. These are heinous crimes and must be punished. However, if you recant and pledge loyalty this very night, we will allow you to return to the village, your families, and your lives. You will be on probation and will be expected to be faithful from this day forth. What say you?"

The villagers were visibly shaken by this pronouncement. They stepped forward one by one, recanted their actions, and pledged loyalty to Self Center.

Expecting a different response from Avery Wan, Euphoria quickly dismissed the four villagers, praising them for their change of heart, and escorted them back to the Village of Subjugation.

Melancholia approached Avery Wan, who was burning with disdain and disgust for these horrible people.

"How can you live with yourselves?" he shouted at them. "You don't deserve anything better than anyone else. You take advantage of, exploit, and oppress the villagers every day. You ask me to recant? You recant! You're the real criminals here."

Sue Perior stood and hissed, "We were hoping you would say that."

Then, they grabbed Avery Wan and dragged him over to the pond behind Self Center. He struggled but could not get free. They lifted him up and threw him into the pond.

The current immediately began to drag him along. He tried to stand but kept slipping on the bottom. Then, he was falling. He had been swept over the falls.

As the leaders returned from the pond, they encountered A Nic Dotal, who had just arrived at Self Center.

"What is going on here? I heard you put some villagers on trial. I met them on the trail. They said that Avery Wan was still here. I would like to speak to him, please."

"He's not here," Sue Perior replied with a smile.

A Nic Dotal noticed that their clothing was wet and torn. These were signs of a struggle. What had they done?

A Nic Dotal had a "punched in the gut" feeling all the way home. *I knew they were dangerous,* A Nic thought. *I didn't think they were murderers. They threw him over the falls. They knew, if they did that, no one would really know what had happened. The swift water would carry the body out to sea. I should have been there. I could have intervened. What now? If I stand up to them, I could have the same fate. A dead person can't help the villagers. Who will be the intermediary who keeps Self Center in check?*

As the years passed, A Nic Dotal lived with regret, while continuing to represent the interests of the villagers. A Nic created useful and whimsical gizmos for the village and used every effort to make the best of the situation on the Island of Status Quo.

N E Wan closed the book and sat in silence. Then, N E rose, placed the tome back into the box, inserted the key, and turned the lock. With key in hand, N E Wan returned to the house.

A Nic Dotal was seated just inside the front door. N E returned the key, which A Nic Dotal donned once again.

"I need time to process all of this," said N E Wan. "I am not sleepy. I couldn't sleep if I wanted to. I need to go somewhere to sort this out."

Rising, A Nic Dotal said, "I know just the place."

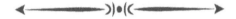

Chapter 11

N E WAN REMOVED the conch shell from the bag, then followed A Nic Dotal out the back door of the house.

"I have created a special place over the years. This is where I come to sort things out. I call it the Garden of Sighs."

Moonlight lit their path as walked a short distance to where the dense foliage opened up to a beautiful garden. N E Wan gasped at the glorious sight.

"I will leave you to your thoughts," said A Nic Dotal, and departed.

N E Wan sat on a bench by a pool. The ambient glow of moonlight made the garden seem a magical place.

Picking up the shell, N E said, "They killed you."

"I wasn't quite sure, but now I know that they did murder me."

"They killed you!"

"Yes."

"I felt as if I was there with you. I share your condemnation of Self Center. I feel the same anger and resentment you felt."

"I realized this as we spoke. I was reliving my experiences along with you."

"Father, what must I do? I have a burning in my soul. I want to stand up for the villagers. I want to help the villagers stand up for themselves. Yet, this group of tyrants is now stronger, more entrenched in their position, and more dangerous than ever."

"Yes, I know. Although I wish it with all my heart, I cannot take this burden from you. This decision is yours and yours alone."

"I have a wonderful life with A Nic Dotal. I have the best of both worlds. Nonetheless, am I betraying myself by continuing to live like this? Not only that, would the villagers even stand up, if given the chance?"

"Some of the villagers were in agreement with me when I sought to bring down Self Center. Yet, when it was all on the line, they recanted and walked away."

"How do I know they will not do the same again?"

N E Wan began to despair and walked throughout the garden. Then, N E returned to the bench and lifted the shell.

The voice began, "People tend to behave with consistency. In making this decision, it is important for you to understand this. You have insight into this situation. You want to help the villagers. You want to impart the knowledge you have gained.

"You come from a different point of view. You want to share this point of view with the people in the village. It is very important to recognize that not everyone responds to new information and different ideas the same way you do. People respond to knowledge differently.

"First of all, we are all ignorant. No one knows everything. The potential for gaining knowledge is seemingly endless. How people respond to their ignorance varies from person to person. Yet, most folks respond to their lack of knowledge in one of three ways.

"The first group responds to ignorance with apathy. They regard a situation that is beyond their experience and understanding with a basic lack of interest. When confronted with a question or paradox, they simply don't care. They find it perfectly acceptable to remain uninformed and ignorant.

"This is mainly because they have neglected to develop a sense of imagination and curiosity in their lives. They do not possess a sense of wonder. They are not inquisitive. If they haven't experienced it directly, they don't have the imagination to even begin to understand it. They do not like to read books, because they lack imagination and have no desire to expand their knowledge. Therefore, attempting to educate them or introduce new ideas to their world is met with their lack of interest.

"A second group responds to ignorance with avoidance. They recognize they lack knowledge of an idea or situation, and they respond by changing the subject or relying on oversimplistic answers. They feel threatened by new ideas. They can become aggressive when faced with a different point of view. They don't want to understand their world. They have an innate fear of the unknown. Instead of being drawn to learn and grow, they avoid it like the plague. They want to pretend the issue doesn't exist.

"This group is drawn to the familiar. They are comforted by habitual patterns and rituals. They appreciate rote teachings that repeat simple solutions. They become afraid and anxious if their accepted reality is questioned. Therefore, attempting to introduce a radical new idea is resisted. The response to their ignorance is to avoid it.

"The third group responds to ignorance with acceptance. They are intrigued when they realize they don't understand something. They long to explore the unknown. They question their world and the status quo. They are curious and imaginative. Instead of being threatened or uncomfortable with ignorance, they actively seek to become less ignorant. This group is generally far less fearful and reactionary. Rather, they are thoughtful. They seek out information. They imagine a different world. They are empowered by embracing knowledge. Therefore, attempting to introduce new ideas to them will be met with enthusiasm and passion."

N E Wan sat quietly, taking all of this in, and then said, "This explains so much. I thought of specific people as you were explaining this. So, if I get what you are saying, I can discover how someone responds to ignorance in their lives by observing how they react to a new idea or to the fact that they don't know something."

"Precisely," said Avery Wan from the shell. "When you see their reaction, then you know whether or not you should continue. Or maybe you should take a different approach with them."

"So, people in the first two groups will never change, no matter what?" asked N E.

"Anyone can change." N E Wan smiled at this. "Oh, I get it," added Avery. "Like I was saying, anyone can change. They must, however, change their conditioned approach to ignorance, in order for that change to become a possibility. This might require much reassurance and hand-holding."

"Does that happen often?" N E asked.

"I have known a few people who were able to change," responded Avery. "But it took a long time and a lot of patience for them to do so."

"Is this what A Nic Dotal is up to?"

"A Nic Dotal is primarily trying to keep Self Center in check," replied Avery. "Self Center would become more dictatorial and tyrannical, if no one was there to stop them. People like A Nic Dotal are essential. A Nic Dotal is also needed to instruct those in the village and find ways to improve their lives."

"I see that," said N E Wan. "I have been working alongside A Nic Dotal, doing those very things. Yet, I don't know if I have the ability to keep my mouth shut. Nor the ability to not do anything and everything I can, to bring Self Center to its knees."

"That was strangely said," Avery retorted. "You should weigh whatever you do or don't do, considering the consequences that will result. You should ask yourself some questions. If you go head-to-head with Self Center, will the villagers rise up with you? If they do not rise up, what will happen to you? What will happen to them? Will your action or inaction serve to make life better? Or worse?

"Simply acting out of revenge or disdain, without considering the possible outcomes, is shortsighted and self-centered in its own right. If you can outsmart them, you might accomplish more lasting change. If you are unable to act in ways that improve the situation, maybe it's better to remove yourself from the situation."

"Are you suggesting that I should leave?" N E asked.

"I am suggesting you should be dead serious about what you are going to do, so you don't end up seriously dead," replied Avery.

N E Wan set the shell down and walked around the garden. Suddenly, all went dark.

N E Wan had been seized, and a bag put over N E's head. N E was bound and then carried away.

Chapter 12

"WELL, THAT WAS easy," came a voice.

"I told you it would be a piece of cake," came the familiar voice of B Trayal.

N E Wan was shocked and afraid. The two strong people who had seized N E were chatting to each other as they carried N E to Self Center.

Soon, N E Wan was stood up and unbound, the bag removed. N E squinted and looked around.

All of the villagers were seated in the square. N E Wan stood before Euphoria, Melancholia, Art Official, Sue Perior, Mister Ection, Miss Demeanour, and B Trayal. The leaders all sported self-satisfied smiles.

Melancholia rose and announced, "N E Wan, you are hereby being charged with sedition, subversion, and inciting a rebellion. These are heinous offenses and will not be tolerated. However, if you will recant and pledge allegiance to Self Center, your punishment will be limited to probation, and you will be free to go. If you refuse, then you will suffer the consequences. What say you?"

N E Wan replied, "If your leadership is legitimate, why do you need to resort to bullying and intimidation? If your ways are right and good, why are you terrified when they are questioned? There is an inherent difference between strength and violence. There is an ethical distinction between legitimacy and brutal subjugation. You brought me here by force because you are afraid. You feel vulnerable because you know I can see through you. You know your ways are immoral and unjust. I am here because I stand as a rebuke to your wickedness."

While N E Wan spoke, the inhabitants of Self Center became agitated, and their smiles turned to sneers. They began gnashing their teeth. Then, they yelled as one and rushed forward to seize N E Wan.

Together, they walked N E to the pool and cast N E Wan deep into the center of the water.

N E flailed, trying to stand but slipping on the pond's bottom. The current began to drag N E toward the edge of the waterfall. As N E tried to swim against the current, N E's hand hit an object. *What was it? A life vest!* N E quickly donned the vest as the water swept over the falls.

N E was dropping and then hit the water below with a slap, descending deep into the pool below. After what seemed an eternity, N E popped to the surface and gasped for air.

As the current swept N E along, the sound of the falls faded into the distance. N E Wan lay back on the vest and floated down the river feet first. Soon, the current lessened, and the river washed into the ocean. NE Wan swam to the shore, where N E could crawl up on the beach.

As N E Wan removed the vest, N E realized, "I survived the falls."

But N E was exhausted. N E Wan fell into a deep sleep.

Suddenly, N E experienced a familiar sensation.

"Is someone poking me with a stick?" N E Wan said aloud.

"You look terrible," answered a familiar voice.

It was still dark, but N E knew who was poking with that stick. N E stood and followed A Nic Dotal to the beach house. There, N E was given water and a change of clothes.

N E Wan drank the secret elixir, washed off the sand, and changed into dry, clean clothes. The elixir had its usual effect.

"You saved me," said N E Wan.

"I told you I would not make the same mistake twice," replied A Nic Dotal.

As they sat together, speaking quietly, the ambient light of day announced the coming dawn.

"I have something to show you," said A Nic Dotal.

They walked down to the shore. There on the beach was a boat. The boat seemed to be stocked and ready for a long journey. A Nic Dotal reached into the boat and retrieved a stick, before presenting it to N E Wan.

"Aww," N E said with a smile. "You made me a stick. Everyone needs a good stick."

A Nic Dotal smiled, too. "You are welcome here. You and I make a great team. Self Center will not be able to touch you now. You survived the waterfall. We may not be able to make drastic changes, but I think we can do much good together. I know you may choose to go. Who wants to stay someplace where they are trying to kill you? I have given you all you need to travel somewhere new."

N E Wan asked, "If I leave, will the new place be any different?"

"I doubt it," answered A Nic Dotal. "People act like people wherever you go. I want you to know that I support whatever decision you make."

N E and A Nic Dotal embraced, then A Nic Dotal walked off into the trees.

N E looked into the boat. Included among the various supplies was the bag of shells. N E Wan removed the conch shell from the bag and listened.

The only thing N E heard was the sound of the sea.

After a moment of reflection, N E Wan cast the shell far into the ocean and then said, "Thank you, Father. Thank you for everything."

N E Wan sat on the edge of the boat. Memories of the people of the village came to mind. So many experiences N E had had on this island. A warm feeling of love arose within N E Wan.

Just then, a large wave crashed on the beach. As the water receded, N E Wan noticed a large shell. It was the largest sand dollar N E had ever seen.

N E picked it up and looked out to the horizon. The sun began to rise.

THE END